Book three- Wagon Road Trilogy

Depth
in the
Shallows

TONY KINTON

Depth in the Shallows

Tony Kinton

Cedar Arrow Publishing
P. O. Box 88
Carthage, MS 39051
www.tonykinton.com

Scripture taken from the King James Version of the Bible.

ISBN: 978-0-9836829-2-9 (print)
ISBN: 978-0-9836829-3-6 (electronic)

Printed in the United States of America
Cedar Arrow Publishing 10/16/2019

www.tonykinton.com

ACKNOWLEDGMENTS

Books are a team effort. This one is no exception.
With that recognition, I offer my sincere thanks to the following:
Mark Bridges; the team at Lightning Source, Nashville;
Benita Chamblee; Ronnie Shepard; Brian Robinson.
And always to Susan. She is quick with encouragement.
To all, thank you.

Tony Kinton

Chapter 1

The Walker Cabin – 1775

Early spring came on a whispered breeze, still chilled but refreshing. Isaac Walker crawled at daybreak from the half-face down by the creek; it had served as his dwelling since the wedding of Anna and Jackson. A squirrel scolded from a tall hickory and shook budding limbs that deposited water droplets on Isaac's face as he looked upward. The hushed gurgle of creek water, the same that had lulled him to sleep the evening before, seemed to announce a new day. Isaac smiled and stretched as he inhaled what he determined was the sweetest and most satisfying breath of his life.

But still he missed Patience. She had been gone a lifetime. It seemed that way to Isaac. How could it feel so long? How could it yet feel like yesterday? Isaac's mind drifted backward. Then to the present. It is good, now. All is well. Even with this heartache.

"Thank you, God." Isaac's customary first words of each day had lost nothing to familiarity. "You have done it again – given us another grand day to live and love. Thank you." Isaac eased to the creek and splashed cool water on his face. Up the hill, the cabin exhibited signs of life as Anna and Jackson threw covers back and began the morning.

"Anna, in the unlikely event that I fail to tell you later, let me start this day by saying I love you." Jackson pulled Anna close, his bare chest resting firmly against her muslin nightgown.

"And I love you. My life is filled with joy and peace." Anna looked deeply into Jackson's eyes. "I am also ready to meet your family."

"Agreed. I am ready for you to meet them. And I must say that I should have been back in Boston before now. I am something other than a rude frontier farmer, you know." He smiled as he touched Anna's cheek gently.

"Oh, I suppose, Mr. Boston Businessman, but I have to admit that you fit the frontier life quite well." Anna jabbed him gleefully with her finger. "I just may have you fully conditioned to life out here."

Jackson looked askance at Anna, his demeanor teasing. "You have conditioned me all right! And I have thoroughly enjoyed the conditioning. Please don't stop. But, we still have to make that trip to Boston."

"We do. We should begin making plans immediately. And no worries, Jackson; I will go gladly with you anywhere." Anna stepped behind a curtain and exchanged the nightgown for a long petticoat and dress. She walked toward the stove and extracted an apron from a peg protruding from a pine log.

*****

"Ho, in the cabin. You two up and stirring?" Isaac stood respectfully on the porch and waited for a reply.

"Come in, Papa. Breakfast will be ready soon." Anna scurried about preparing bear bacon and fresh eggs. Jackson set aside his journal, moved to the hearth and took a pot from its hook over the fire.

"Coffee, Isaac?" Jackson was already pouring a black stream of the hot brew into a copper cup.

"Yes, please. And thank you. This magic liquid will surely get the blood flowing and joints loosened in even an old man like me." Isaac grinned and reached for the cup.

"Oh hush up, Isaac. You are not old. As I've told you before, you are just right. And Widow Wallace feels the same as I do about that." Anna partially turned from the stove, her eyes dancing with mischief as she glanced at Isaac. "Not another word about your age. Just drink your coffee in silence." Anna let her eyes meet Jackson's, and the two of them chuckled softly.

"Marybeth again, is it? When are you going to leave me be about her?" Isaac made another unsuccessful attempt to assuage their suspicions regarding his obvious attraction for Marybeth Wallace.

"Never, Isaac." Jackson poured himself a cup of the hot coffee. "If you ask me, it is about time you dress in something other than those dirty buckskins, go to the settlement, get down on your knees and do your best to convince Marybeth Wallace that she should marry you."

"I don't recall asking you, Mr. Bain." Isaac took a sip of coffee, the steam from which rising with such ferocity that he had to squint his eyes. He sighed. "But since you mention it, Marybeth is a fine woman. A man would do well to win her hand."

"That he would, Papa. And you are wasting time; you should have already proposed to Marybeth."

"But I still miss Patience dreadfully."

"As do I." Anna glanced over her shoulder in the direction of her father. "But Papa, she is gone That is out of your control. Life is best lived if we move on to love again."

"Perhaps." Isaac stumbled as if he were exhibiting agreement with that last statement.

"Papa, I know. There is a hole in my heart as well. But love, Isaac; it helps mend the broken pieces. Now you two contrary gentlemen get over here and eat breakfast. Jackson, ask a blessing, please." Anna's pleasantness permeated the entire cabin as Jackson and Isaac obliged her request.

"Isaac, Anna and I need to discuss a matter with you." Jackson spoke gently, knowing that Isaac would experience a touch of grief brought on by their leaving for Boston.

"Yes, of course. I'm sure this is about your need to go back home and tend to business."

"That it is. I had hoped to be there by now. No regrets on staying here since the wedding, but I must make firm plans for the trip as quickly as possible. And I naturally want Anna to go with me." Jackson watched Isaac fumble with his coffee cup and hang his head.

"Oh, I understand. You two must go. Please, do so with no concern for me. I will miss you both terribly, but I will make it fine. I can handle spring planting and the summer work with ease. When do you plan to leave?"

"I would think within the week." Sun poured himself another cup of coffee. Anna turned from her routine of clearing the table and entered the conversation.

"Is that what you are thinking, Sun? Say by the 5th of this month?"

"Yes. I can make arrangements quickly. Let's set a departure time for this upcoming Friday." Sun was resolute but still showed his obvious concern for Isaac.

"I'll assist in any way I can." Isaac set his cup down on the hearth. "Are you thinking of taking a wagon or going horseback?"

"The wagon would be more comfortable for such a long trip, but horseback would be quicker. Anna, what do you think?" Sun reached out and took Anna's hand, pulling her close and clearly making her a participant in the decision making.

"I agree. " Anna put her arm around Sun's waist. "My suggestion, if I may, is to do both. Let's consider taking a wagon and trail two saddle horses behind. Since we will have to camp at nights along the way, we can put a few supplies and a canvas covering in the wagon. If we have to at some point, we can livery the wagon and team at a settlement or with a family and hasten the remaining travel on the saddle horses."

"That sounds logical." Sun smiled at his wife. "I'll ride to the settlement today and locate a solid team of draft horses. I will also go to the blacksmith shop and talk with Mr. Rodrick. He was building a new wagon the last time I was there. Perhaps it's finished by now. And I'll have him make an extra wheel if he doesn't have one on hand. Oh, and if I come back without a bucket of grease for the axles, remind me to get that when we go back through the settlement the day we leave."

"I will do that, Sun. But I'm sure you will remember." Anna flashed her approval of her husband's attention to detail.

"It's set, then. You two will leave Friday morning." Isaac looked first at Anna and then at Sun. "I'll begin putting together some jerked meat and dried beans for you. And I'll get two water kegs mounted on the sides of the wagon when you get back here with it. Maybe there won't be one of those troublesome spring snows. If not, you should have pleasant weather."

"That we should, Isaac. And thank you for your help." Sun Bain held his father-in-law in high esteem. Snowball, now much more than a pup, whined at the door and eagerly waited for someone to come out and pat her perfectly proportioned head. She, too, would miss Anna and Sun.

*****

"I'm just wondering." Isaac waited until he and Sun stepped outside to continue the conversation. "What do you think the situation is with the British? Last I heard it seems war is on the horizon. I don't suppose you and Anna will run into trouble?" Snowball danced and yapped and ran in tight circles around the two men, joyful to have some company there in the bright sunshine.

"Well, I have thought about that. Obviously, I can't be certain about anything, but I conclude that since I am not a part of any colonial militia or rebelling group, I, we, will be of little consequence to any British forces we might encounter. And even if we do encounter them, it won't be until we are in or very near Boston. There should be no significant issues with that. Be assured, Isaac, that I will be judicious in every move. I will take care of your daughter."

"I know you will, Sun. I trust you completely. It's just that Anna will be so far from home and things are terribly unsettled. I can't help but entertain a shadow of worry. That is what a father does – worries about his daughter. And his son-in-law in this case. But I do trust God. I know He will be right beside you."

"And so do I, Isaac. I have concern and I trust God. We will be more than careful, and please know that we will miss you and the frontier while we are away." Snowball came to Sun's side, a stick in her mouth and excitement in her eyes. "And yes, Snowball; we will miss you as well. You take good care of Isaac." Sun tossed the stick and Snowball ran to retrieve it.

"You best be on your way to check on that wagon and team. Anna and I will see to things here."

"Yes, of course. I'll go inside and tell Anna to expect me back here no later than tomorrow evening. I'll see you then, Isaac."

"Yes, then." Isaac turned and started toward an aging hickory on the hillside. He went there often.

Chapter 2

Boston

"Rebecca, please, I must have a word with you." William Clarkson stood at the door of the Bomar House. Rebecca had opened that door with haste when she learned it was William there to see her, and she bubbled with enchanted excitement as she looked into his eyes. That jubilance faded quickly, however. William's countenance was not that of a suitor intent upon asking for Rebecca's hand. It was resolute, foreign, distracted. Rebecca recoiled in shock.

"Yes, of course. Come in, William. Please, let's go to the parlor so that we can talk." They moved inside and sat close but were rigid and contemplative. The gravity of this situation disturbed them both.

"Rebecca, I have been thinking and praying about a matter of great import for more than a month now. I very much regret that my decision is going to alarm you, but I must do what I have chosen to do."

William Clarkson's mind began to spin, a maple leaf on an autumn breeze, his thoughts jumbled, disconnected, his heart in two places, two pieces at once, neither place nor piece supplying enough blood to sustain living – or so it felt. The prejudicial decision, this urgent decision, one which he could not make but must make - had made already. With this decision, life, everything, would be different, beginning right now. Would there be any redemption in either route available to him?

"William, no. Please, no. Is it me? What have I done? Have I been too forward and perhaps a bit too eager in our relationship? Please, tell me what I have done." And like William's, Rebecca's mind was caught up in turbulence, a whirling wind, angry lightning, a roar and rumble that muted all sounds, that curtailed, at least almost, her breathing.

"Oh, Rebecca. No; you have done nothing to bring about this decision."

"Still, you are going to sit there and tell me you are breaking our relationship, that perhaps you choose to find someone else or have already found someone else or don't want anyone or whatever it is?" She didn't know what she was saying; she just had to say and keep saying and somehow avoid his response, be it benign or terminal. "How could you, William?"

"No, Rebecca." William Clarkson took her hand and held it tightly. What he feared, what had blinded him with dread, unfolded into a reality he did not want to face. But that decision. He had made a decision. "It is not you. And never could I want nor need anyone else. You are the light of my life; I love you with all my being. You will never have legitimate cause to fear my breaking our relationship. But this decision will, I am keenly aware, concern you and perhaps bring you pain. For that I feel sincere regret."

"Well, tell me. What is this all about?"

"Rebecca, war is coming. Recent actions suggest that. Men are preparing to take up arms. Rebecca, I must become one of those. I can't hold my head high if I sit back enjoying the pleasantries of life I have come to know with you and fail to rise to the occasion of defending our freedom. That is not who and what I am. I must enlist and serve in any way I can. That is the matter I want to address with you."

"No, William. Please. You can't do this. What if something happens to you? What if you are maimed or killed? What am I to do? No; you simply must not do this." Tears were now flowing down Rebecca's cheeks, her hands trembling. She extracted that hand William held in his and slid away to create some distance between them. She, at this moment, was not fond of this man, this stranger. "I won't allow it."

"Rebecca, please. Allow me to...."

"No! I'll not hear of it, William. I can't lose you. This foolish action you propose is out of the question. You will not go to war."

"But...."

"No, William. No. Now I will thank you to leave me alone; I must have some time to compose myself." Rebecca stood, her eyes still flooded with tears and a grimace distorting her otherwise beautiful face. She turned abruptly and walked from the room. William sat stunned, unsure of what would transpire. He had expected some reaction. But this? He feared it, somewhere deep within the recesses of his being. Again – but this? He, too, stood and let himself out, stepping into the sunshine of an early-spring afternoon in Boston.

*****

Frontier

Isaac Walker was at the big hickory again. Snowball and a crude marker his only companions. "Good afternoon, Patience." There was a tiny breeze. Was it friend or foe? Was it a portent of life or death? He remembered: *thankless days of indenture; slow progress to Yadkin*

Valley, one horse, a small wagon, Anna, Patience, a skinny pup named Snowball – not this Snowball, the one before this one; laughter; love. "You never complained." Salty tears assaulted his cheeks. Big ones. But still, "Thank you, Lord. You have blessed me."

*****

Boston

"Rebecca, please come in." Richard Bomar opened the door of his handsomely-appointed office and reached to embrace his daughter. "Is it permissible to hug you?"

"Of course, Father. Always. I still need your hugs just as much as when I was your little girl." The two stood in warmth and shared connection, Richard detecting tears on Rebecca's cheeks. "I am pleased that you could see me. I know you are busy."

"I'm never too busy to see my favorite daughter." Richard gestured to a plush, ornate sofa.

"Your only daughter." Rebecca postured a faint smile.

"Tears are a part of life; I gladly share yours." Richard Bomar's gentle words reduced Rebecca to heavy sobs.

"Thank you, Papa. Your words are always gentle and perfect." Rebecca coaxed her response from the midst of consuming pain.

"And never wasted on you, Rebecca. You are the joy of my life." Richard tipped her chin upward and looked into her eyes. "What ache deep inside is causing this agony?"

"Oh, Papa; it is William. You know I love him with all my being. As I love you, but just in a different way. I mean…."

"I know what you mean, Rebecca. So please feel free to omit explanation and allow me to help carry your burden. What is wrong with William?"

"Other than a foolish decision he has reached, there is absolutely nothing wrong with William. Nothing at all. He is perfect. Or at least until this. Now he has launched a campaign of destruction."

"A campaign of destruction?" A quizzical concern showed on Richard's face as he pronounced those words slowly and with enhanced diction. "My, Rebecca. What could William have done to produce such a proclamation as that? You love him; he loves you. What is this all about?"

"He is enlisting to take up arms in this frivolous conflict with the Mother Country. In essence, he has disregarded my wishes." Rebecca fell silent; Richard found himself minus the proper words for an understanding reply.

"Disregarded your wishes?"

"Yes. I told him I would not allow such inconsiderate action, that it was forbidden. I told him I would hear nothing of it."

"Well, I suppose William now knows how you feel about this matter!"

"He does, but he still insists on enlisting and taking up arms. I will not have it, Papa. How could he do this to me?" Rebecca allowed a scowl to distort her otherwise radiant countenance.

"Rebecca, I am terribly sorry. I know you are hurting and afraid. Perhaps somewhat angry and disappointed. You may even feel abandoned and betrayed. Natural, human responses, these are. I hurt for and with you. We must, however look at the entire set of circumstances; we must consider reality and trust God fully."

"The circumstances are that this war is a futile effort, and the reality is that William has acted in a fashion contrary to my wishes and has turned his back on me."

"Really?" Richard ached with the awareness that he was forcing Rebecca to analyze the situation with a depth that went much farther than emotion. He struggled for gentleness. Rebecca raised an eyebrow and tilted her head in growing trepidation.

"Yes, really. What else could it be other than open rebellion against my judgement?"

"Rebecca, I love you." Richard took her hand and held it softly. "I would never intentionally do anything to hurt you or jeopardize our relationship. I care deeply for both you and William; I wish all the best for you two. But I must be honest in this discussion and pray that any advice I proffer comes with the wisdom that only God can give."

"Oh yes, Father; do be honest. Just like William was honest. Honesty seems to come with ease from men who have reached a decision made without concern for others." Rebecca was visibly angered and allowed her frustration to burst full grown onto her father.

"Honesty should come with ease to all who follow God's word, but along with it should be that concern you mention. Can you be sure William made his decision before considering you? I find that difficult to believe."

"Oh, I suppose he gave it some thought, for he told me what he was about to do would probably bring me pain."

"So he did show concern for you?"

"Perhaps, but he would not change his mind even after I forbade him from following through with his nonsense."

"Forbade him, Rebecca?"

"I told him he simply could not do it."

"Does genuine love give us permission to forbid?"

"Well, I suppose it does. It depends upon what we are forbidding."

"Perhaps. But be careful with that thinking, Rebecca. Where are the boundaries of that forbidding? Can they be restricted to hostility or ill treatment or neglect, which likely demands forbiddance, or do they subtly creep into less consequential elements of living? Can forbidding in one avenue of grave import infiltrate those lesser elements and become the ordinary? Simply allowing a wrong and harmful practice to become familiar and accepted as the norm in no way makes it right. So please, as I just said, be careful."

"So are you saying I should let William continue while I remain silent in this matter?"

"Not at all. You are clearly justified in voicing your opinion. And certainly you are justified in expressing your concern. You love William and naturally fear any threat that could take him from you. But I do think that failing to discuss this more in depth and allowing William to share his feelings completely regarding this decision could be in error. Doing so could create a chasm that neither of you could ever cross."

"But, Father, I am not being unreasonable. I am just watching out for William."

"You may view it that way, Rebecca." Richard paused in reflection.

"But what, Papa?"

"But…."

"Yes?"

"What I need to point out hurts me, Rebecca."

"Pease continue."

"As you wish."

"I wish, Papa. Now what do you have to say?"

"In your conversation I heard your use of "I," "me" and "my" a great many times. And they were all directed toward what you expected or forbade or felt. William was mentioned only in the context of what he is doing to you. Is it possible that what he is doing is for and not to you?" Richard fell silent and studied Rebecca's downcast demeanor.

"No. That is not possible. Not possible at all."

"Can you be sure, Rebecca? Did you fully hear William out

regarding this matter?"

"Oh, I heard quite enough. Quite enough, indeed. William is showing an obstinate side of himself I never knew existed."

"Is that true, Rebecca? Have you forgotten that time William resigned his position at Bomar Mercantile because he felt his independence was threatened and elected to make his way in another direction? Do you remember that?"

"Well, yes. But this is different."

"Different?"

"Yes, different. This time he is going against my wishes, and this is far more serious."

"And your wishes then were for him to leave Bomar Mercantile?"

"Of course not. I wanted him to stay."

"But he didn't stay. He left. He did what he felt he had to do. But it worked out well in the end. You surely saw and recognized William's resilience and self-reliance then. Is this so different?"

"Well, yes and no. Father, this could be a matter of life and death."

"That it could, Rebecca. But death is always a possibility for the living. If we live only in an effort to avoid the threat of death, I conclude we hardly live at all."

"Yes, but…."

"Rebecca, it just may be possible that William has given this far more thought than you imagine. It could be that he has agonized over this entire matter and has come to realize that you, he, all people deserve freedom. His decision may have sprung from his love for you, not some blatant disregard as you see it. Could it be he has chosen to take up arms because of you?"

"I don't…. I…."

"Look around us, Rebecca. We are not free; we are not at peace.

Boston is in turmoil. We are under persecution of a distant ruler who blinks at our petitions and disregards our input. The colonists may not be able to avert military conflict. Commerce is suffering, and that means people are suffering. We are being taxed in exorbitant fashion with no one to represent us. There is likely no solution other than to break from the Mother Country and establish our own government. William, I would say, has come to realize this. I am truly sorry, Rebecca, but the time has come for struggle. A sad and tragic position for us all. I am sorry."

"And so am I, Papa. So am I."

*****

March 23, 1775, Patrick Henry took the floor with a rousing speech at a Richmond church. He concluded with words that would live in history: "I know not what course others may take, but as for me, give me liberty or give me death."

On the night of April 18, 1775, Paul Revere's echoed shouts spread across the Massachusetts countryside from Charlestown to Lexington. The British were marching from Boston to take over the colonial arsenal at Concord. They, however, encountered heavy resistance. At Lexington Green, 77 local minutemen, as well as others, met the force of 700 British. It is unclear who fired the first shot, but the melee ended with eight Americans lost.

Later at Concord, the British met hundreds of willing opponents and were forced to retreat to Boston. These first battles of the war cost 273 British and 90 Americans their lives.

Chapter 3

The Road to Boston

The trip had been pleasant for Anna and Sun to this point. They had stopped in various settlements along the way, had made new acquaintances and had slept peacefully under the stars most nights. Save three evenings of rain, these never consecutive, they had not even needed the canvas shelter.

"I'm glad you thought to bring that along," Anna had teased on the first night of downpours. "You would have had a soaked and contentious wife had you not." They had snuggled closely and laughed with abandon as the skies scowled and rain pattered.

"We are making good time," Sun noted as they progressed toward their destination. "Boston is not far now. I can hardly wait to see my family there and have them meet you and you them. I will introduce you proudly as the grand treasure you are."

"Goodness, Sun. Stop the flattery. You will have me thinking too highly of myself." Anna's eyes sparkled as she spoke.

"No flattery; only truth. And you could never be of the temperament that would lead to a misplaced perception of who and what you are. You are too humble and gracious for such nonsense. Believe me, you are more than worthy of my accolades."

"Thank you, Sun. You are most kind and loving. I am fully pleased to be your wife."

And then a rider, coming at a hard gallop around the bend ahead.

"You there." The rider jerked his horse to a stop beside the wagon, the horse's eyes wide and nostrils flared, great gulps of air rushing through them in an effort to replenish the supply expended. "You heading for Boston?"

"We are. And what is the cause of your hurry?" Sun was curious and exhibited trepidation at this one's sudden and boisterous intrusion. He put his hand on the grip of a flintlock pistol set securely in his sash.

"Things are a bit unsettled back there. I'm off to relay a message of the situation." The rider was out of breath.

"Unsettled?" Sun snapped to attention at the pronouncement.

"You haven't heard I guess. A British force of 700 left Boston and marched toward the armory in Concord. They met a few of our men on Lexington Green and killed eight of them. Simple murder if you ask me. But when the Brits got to Concord, the story changed. There were hundreds of our brave ones waiting, and they put those outsiders on the run back to Boston. The Redcoats now believe we can and will fight. What we have here is a revolution and not just some incidental rebellions."

Sun's mouth dropped open in shock. "I had heard there was trouble but had no idea it had escalated to this."

"Well, it has. Talk is George Washington will be named Commander-in-Chief, and it appears a full-blown Continental Army is in the making. You two can get into the city, but be careful with every move. You'll see more than your share of Redcoats everywhere you look."

The rider then spurred his horse and burst down the road, shirt flapping in rhythm with the horse's gait as he bounced out of sight. Anna and Sun sat in silence, searching for words as they processed this alarming account.

"I was afraid this would be the outcome." Sun finally broke a haunting hush. "There was just too much discord between the colonies and King George to expect anything short of war."

"What should we do, Sun?" Anna's voice revealed that she was deeply shaken. "War. Even the word spells tragedy, no matter the outcome."

"It does. But war seems inevitable under certain conditions. This is likely one of them. If no resolution can be reached otherwise, the colonies must sever ties with the King. All of us deserve to be free and allowed to pursue life as we feel led. No far-removed government should have the right to infringe on the liberties we seek."

"Yes, of course. I trust you in this, Sun."

"Thank you. I must say, however, that I am not the final authority and I certainly don't know what will transpire in all this. But I do have faith that God has put us here for His purpose, and we must be diligent in doing what He calls us to do. People should be free. Our only true freedom comes through Jesus, but freedom to choose and live life unencumbered by an overbearing task master is something worth pursuing, even if that pursuit means war."

"I understand, and I support you in such matters. I, too, want to be free, whether in Boston or on the frontier. Isaac instilled that in me. Freedom. It is worth the struggle."

Chapter 4

The Frontier

"I miss them, Snowball." Isaac Walker patted the dog's head as she whined and looked across the landscape. "I know you do, too."

Though little more than a month had passed since Anna and Sun set off toward Boston, it seemed much longer for Isaac and Snowball. Summer was now winning its struggle to claim the frontier, and that familiar humidity caused one to dread August. Isaac wiped his brow against a bulbous sleeve of his long shirt. He stood, demeanor pensive and eyes searching for something; he was not sure what, but he was searching.

"Snowball." She cocked her head inquisitively and perked her ears to attention. "I've been thinking about Marybeth." Snowball wagged her tail at the gentleness of his voice. "I think Anna and Sun are right; I have been wasting time. I should give serious thought to approaching Marybeth about marriage. What do you think of that?" Snowball whined as if she understood and wanted to express her approval.

"Since things are quiet here and work is not pushing, I think

I'll go to the settlement and call on Marybeth. Is that okay with you, girl?" The dog looked curiously at Isaac and hassled. Temperatures were reaching toward unpleasant, even for the animals. "Tomorrow, then. I'll go talk with Marybeth. But you need to stay here and guard for me. Will you do that?" Snowball barked approvingly.

*****

"We have both experienced loss, Marybeth." Isaac spoke gently in his conclusion of their discussion about losing their spouses. "It was tragic, as life often is. But we move on."

"That we do, Isaac. And we must not attempt to live in the past. That is simply an unwise use of the time God has given us." Marybeth gave every indication of her willingness to move forward in all avenues of living. In fact, she had already exhibited that through her involvement with the community and the church family in the settlement. The loss of her husband and Isaac's wife was years behind.

"You mentioned age, Isaac. You are still young, particularly in my eyes. And the years that separate the two of us are of no great importance. A decade is insignificant when considered in the whole of life. Please, think nothing of something that is no real obstacle." Isaac stood from his chair in the presence of Marybeth and knelt quietly before her.

Then troubling thoughts: *I must talk with Patience about this. I have talked with Patience about this. Often. Why these monsters of doubt, of fear, of something that even looks like regret? Why? I should propose marriage to Marybeth. I should get busy about living, loving, sharing. But Patience? She is gone. I love Patience. I love Marybeth. How? Should I do this? Can I legitimately do anything other than this?* Troubling thoughts. Then peace.

"Marybeth, I have grown to care for you deeply; you, I believe, share the same sentiments for me. We live by the same values and have had ample opportunity to develop a relationship. A relationship that adds even more meaning and purpose to my life. I come to you now as a humble, frontier man who treasures your companionship. Marybeth, will you be my wife?"

"Isaac Walker, I thought you would never ask." Marybeth spoke without hesitancy. "Of course I will be your wife, and gladly I must say. You have fully captured my heart. Nothing would make me happier than to spend the remainder of my life with you. You are dear and precious, a kind and loving man who offers respect to others and follows God daily. Yes, I will be proud to become Mrs. Isaac Walker."

Isaac, still kneeling cupped Marybeth's hand in his and smiled, tears of joy trickling down his weathered cheeks. "I love you, Marybeth."

*****

The Edge of Boston

"Halt!" A shout echoed from the roadside as a dozen British soldiers burst into view and stood at attention shoulder-to-shoulder, blocking the route. Their Brown Bess muskets, complete with mounted bayonets portrayed a menacing image as they glistened in generous sunshine, sunshine that spoke more appropriately of peace than war. "State your intent."

Then Sun remembered: *that night of the vicious attack on the frontier; that arrow that almost cost him his life; that startling explosion of black powder in the pan of his .54; that sickening thud of the round ball contacting flesh and bone; that brief but horrid expression on the face of a brave young man as he fell backward from the impact.* Sun remembered.

And he remembered more: *Anna's gentle care; his own madness brought by fevered infection; his pronouncement of his love for Anna even when he was in marauding anesthesia. He really didn't actually remember that, but Anna told him. He believed her. And he remembered her distance, rejection even, when he was found out, when he had to admit his falsehood even if it had been innocent. It was, after all, a lie. He remembered most her acceptance of his proposal. And she sat right here beside him now.*

"And what gives you the right to ask our intent?" Jackson Bain was incensed. This was his first encounter with a truly hostile and potentially dangerous enemy - apart from that tragic event on the frontier several months prior of course. The nauseous chill of battle and death flitted about his heart and mind like a flock of starlings.

"We, Sir, are under no obligation to explain our rights to ask anything of you. You are British subjects and we represent the King. You would do well, Sir, to oblige and forthwith proclaim your intent as requested." The Officer in charge spoke in a polite but demanding British accent, measured protocol guiding his response. "Now if you will be so kind, Sir. What is your intent?"

Then thoughts: Sun was inert, smothered in consternation, filled with confusion. *Anna. I must protect Anna. How? This man is bad. What is bad? What is good? Is one man's life experience, an experience apart from another man's, sufficient to require the designation bad? And allegiance. What part might that play? Two different men; two different persuasions. Good; bad?* Sun finally spoke.

"I answer under protest, Sir. I am Jackson Bain; this is my wife Anna. We are going to visit my mother, sisters and their families." Sun was curt, perfunctory.

"And what of your load there?" The Officer gestured to the wagon and its contents.

"That, Sir, is of no consequence." Sun felt his anger rising but

23

resolved to keep it from erupting and worsening this interrogation. "A few simple supplies for the trail. A piece of canvas to be used in the event of rain. Some clothes. Look if you must."

"Nothing that pertains to this ridiculous and futile attempt at revolution that you subjects will surely regret?" There was a restrained but noticeable stir of amusement among the troops at the Officer's question.

"Nothing. And we shall wait to see if this revolution is ridiculous or futile, Sir." Sun found it difficult to contain himself, but Anna's presence and the possibility of being charged with some fabricated infraction weighed heavily on him. "Now if you will excuse us, we shall be on our way as we were." Sun gathered the reins in his hands and prepared to coax the horses forward.

"As you wish, Sir. But I advise you to be more supportive of the Crown and show its due respect. You colonists would do well to abandon this senseless debacle. The King will not be subjugated to rude behavior minus severe retribution." The Officer and his troops stepped aside, their rigidity firmly unaltered.

*****

The Frontier

"Snowball; where are you, girl?" The dog came yapping from the creek, her excitement overflowing at Isaac's arrival from his trip to the settlement. "There you are." Isaac cuffed her ears and ran his fingers down her back and sides as she licked his face, a face now hosting three days of unshaven stubble. "She said yes, Snowball. Marybeth said she would marry me." The dog, bubbling with enthusiasm ran in tight circles about Isaac, her back legs appearing to speed ahead of her front. Dust flew in her wake. Isaac smiled.

Chapter 5

The Bain House

The Bain household was astir. News had reached Martha Bain a few minutes earlier, and she busied herself with tidying up. "I don't want to meet my new daughter-in-law with this place amuck." Martha allowed her thought to take words. A maid fluttered about and spread a fresh white cloth on the dining table.

"All will be well, Mam. Your house is never amuck. And I know you are excited about Mr. Jackson and his bride. I look forward to seeing them myself." Louise was a long-time and dedicated employee of the household.

"Thank you, Louise. I don't know what I would do without your assistance. I appreciate you more than you can know."

"I know, Mam. You are always quick to express your gratitude for my work and for me. And I don't know what I would do without you, Mam. Your kindness over the years has been a bright spot in my life."

"Mutual, then, I would say. Let's stay busy and get this place looking as it should." Martha dusted a chair while Louise did the same for the big mantle. She smiled at Martha's elevated spirit, obvious in her hurried steps and fussing over the house. "They should be here soon."

"As you wish, Mam. Everything will be spotless. But it is always spotless!"

*****

George Washington, appointed Commander-in-Chief June 16, had written to his wife from Philadelphia weeks earlier. He noted that he would within minutes of the writing be leaving for the camp in Boston and doubted his ability to get a letter to her until arrival there. When that arrival would be, he did not know. The Commander expressed his faith in the Providence that had been fully bountiful to him thus far. He also reminded Martha of his entire affection for her and asked she give his love to other members of the family. While hope remained that war could be avoided, the next few months would prove otherwise.

*****

"There they are, Louise! There they are!" Martha Bain could not contain herself. She rushed on aging legs from the house and onto the steps outside, tears already evident in her yet bright eyes, these made even more so by the return of Jackson.

"Sun; Sun. My dear Sun." Martha gathered him in her arms and sobbed with joy. Jackson returned the embrace and shed euphoric tears of his own.

"Mother. My dear Mother. Oh how I have missed you terribly." Sun pushed her to arm's length to look into her very heart. "I wanted to get back a month earlier but was unable to do so." Sun then took

Anna's hand and pulled her close.

"And Mother, allow me to introduce you to my beautiful and gracious wife. Mother, this is Anna Walker, Anna Bain now. Anna, I present to you the most wonderful mother one could ever imagine, Martha Bain."

The two most significant women in Sun's life stood speechless. It was as if neither could find the proper words. "Sun, she is all you said she was." Martha finally broke the spell that had seemed momentarily to bind them. "Dear, dear Anna. Welcome to the Bain family." Martha clutched Anna in a sincere and warm embrace that portrayed acceptance. "It is so very good to finally meet you."

"And to meet you, Mrs. Bain. I feel as I have known you for some time now. Jackson is seldom short of words when it comes to praise for you."

"Now, now, dear. You don't mean to tell me you believe everything this romantic poet you married tells you, do you? And please, it is Martha. Mrs. Bain is not necessary."

"Thank you. Martha it is, and I already feel a part of this family. I love your son completely and look forward to the days we all have ahead of us. Family. That is the key to happiness. It is, second only to my relationship with God, the most important thing in my life."

"You speak well and with conviction, Anna. And I must tell you that I could hear no more welcome words than those you just spoke. Again, welcome. Now you two come inside. Louise has tea waiting. Jacob will stable your horses and put the wagon away." A celebration of renewal had begun.

*****

Yadkin Settlement

"Can't help but worry a mite 'bout the boy and Miss Anna." Simon Keats had hardly stopped talking about them since the wedding and his and Nora Jean's return to their cabin in the settlement. "'Spect all's well with 'em, but still a touch worried."

"Put your mind at ease, Simon." Nora Jean ruffled her fingers through Simon's scruffy hair and brushed his weathered cheek, now clean shaven and sparkling from a solid scrubbing. "God has little place for worry in His plans. Jackson is healthy, intelligent and especially wise for a man his age. He has a precious and dedicated wife, and both of them have a personal relationship with Jesus. So tell me: What is there to worry about, Simon?"

"Oh, I reckon ain't nothin' of no real consequence. It's just that I done invested all this time and learnin' in that boy and shorely would hate to see him go and foul things somehow. He could use some ever-day lessons in keepin' them smartsomes in order, and ain't nobody more smartsome than Simon Keats to help him hone them rough edges." Simon set free that roaring laughter with which everyone in his company knew well.

"So that's it, is it? You are not so much worried about Anna and Jackson as you are in having no one to whom you can impart your smartsomes. Is that it, Simon?" Nora Jean stood with hands on hips and stared gently into Simon's eyes.

"Oh, now hold on there, Nora Jean. Simon Keats ain't never been one to meddle and give advice where advice weren't needed. No sirreeee. Always been one to keep kinda' quiet like and let the other feller do his own dealins'. Shorely never been one to get into the business of somebody who didn't want me there."

"As you have said on countless occasions, Simon. But what about meddling in Isaac's business with Marybeth? Or Jackson's business with Anna? Or any other of a long list which comes to mind? What about that?" Nora Jean was persistent.

"Well now, you gotta' understand. Them situations you just

brought to mind waren't done in meddlin'. They was all proper times for some good-sense talkin'. And I'd a' busted iffin I hadn't a' jumped right in there and told the truth of the whole matter. 'Sides, look at how them things all turned out. Just 'bout perfect iffin you ask me."

"Well, I suppose I'll have to give you that, Simon. Things did turn out splendidly. But you were still meddling."

"Maybe a little, Nora Jean. But I done told you 'bout my smart-somes and how somebody needs to be around with the right thinkin.'"

"Yes, yes. Whatever you say, Somon. And while we are on the subject, what has happened to that effort of revising your way of talking? You were doing well, and now you have slipped right back into that long hunter babble. What do have to say for yourself?"

"I thought we's talkin' 'bout my meddlin' and not my speechin.'"

"I'm not sure speechin' is a word, and since we were getting nowhere with my chastisement of your meddlesome ways, I elected to change the subject." Nora Jean smiled at her obvious success of moving Simon to other matters.

"Well, 'spect a woman's got the right to change things iffin she wants. And Nora Jean, you ain't never gonna change so much as to make me not plumb full of love for you. Shorely ain't. You done grabbed a' hold of my heart and I ain't gonna let you let go of that hold."

"Sweet, Simon. And never would I want to let go. You hold my heart as well, even if you do talk in the manner of long hunters. And please don't worry about Anna and Jackson. They will be fine."

"Well said, Mrs. Keats. And thank you. But may I maintain a slight measure of proper concern for the Bain Family?"

"That you may and that you should. You do well with that. Oh, and Simon, thank you for speaking as I know you can!"

Chapter 6

Bain House

The house overflowed with family and friends, all present
to greet Jackson and Anna. A long table held impressive servings
of roast pork, turkey, pastries and fruit. Rum was available for the
asking. In a distant corner of the parlor, a string quartet alternated
between John Valentine minuets and British folk tunes. Some guests
held tightly to their big goblets and sang along on occasion, swaying
in rhythm to familiar melodies.

At some point, determined and understood only by Martha
Bain, she eased near the quartet and whispered to the violinist. An
excerpt from Handel's "Water Music" then filled the room, gradually
causing all to fall silent, attention fully focused on sonorous sound.
Following a sustained chord that pronounced finality, Martha gained
the floor.

"Friends and family, welcome." Martha's voice was strong,
resolute, belying her declining health and increasing years. "I have
not adequate words to express my appreciation for your presence and
kindness. This gathering is greatly enhanced by your gracious partic-

ipation. Few things in life could bring me more pleasure than what we are doing here this fine evening." A cheer, first reserved but soon unfurled with abandon, rose from the guests. They applauded and nodded in deference to Martha Bain, a pillar of grace and cordiality.

"Why we have met here this evening is no secret. We have come to celebrate. Some might say that celebration is not in order in these often dismal days of uncertainty, but I contend that not only is it in order, it is paramount. God is still in control and is still blessing all of us. I am particularly blessed this evening, for I have my son back here with me." Eyes turned to Jackson; smiles greeted him.

"But I dare not stop with that proclamation. You will see standing there beside him his wife, my daughter-in-law, Anna. I present to all you Anna Walker Bain." Cheers returned, this time more boisterous and jubilant than before. Guests encircled the newlyweds. Men offered Jackson handshakes and slaps on the back and afforded Anna courteous bows. Women hugged Anna and admonished Jackson to be the husband he should be. Some frowned and wagged a menacing finger near his nose before exploding into congratulatory smiles. Impending war was far from the minds of those in attendance.

"But please, if I may have your attention." Martha struggled to reign in the joviality. "You know my daughters Cora and Cassie and their husbands Robert and Jonathan." The crowd acknowledged the Jamisons and Richardsons. "And you are aware that Cora and Robert lost their little Alice in that tragic fire." The room became suddenly hushed. Specifics of that fire had been the subject of whispered gossip since Squire Bain's death, and never had any member of the Bain family spoken of it in public. Yet, here was Martha addressing it for all to hear.

"Sorrow and hurt come in intolerable bundles at times, and that is what we all experienced in that fire. Details are still shadowed, but we all, I am sure, know full well the truth of it. But we must also recognize that it is not only in the past but was then and is now out or our control. We move forward, always trusting in God to extract the good from the bad. And I am pleased to say this evening that is exactly what He has done. Cora, Robert, forgive me if I infringe upon your privacy, but I think I shall explode if I don't tell everyone. Friends and family, I am to be a new grandmother. Cora and Robert are expecting a child!"

*****

Frontier Settlement

"Should we wait for Anna and Jackson to return, Marybeth?" Isaac Walker was eager to begin a new life with Marybeth, but to consider doing so minus the presence of Anna caused him alarm. "I know she is aware of my feelings for you and is in full support of any decisions we make regarding our lives, but it seems unfitting to have a wedding without her here, along with Jackson, of course. What do you think, Marybeth?"

"I think I am deeply in love with you, Isaac and am completely prepared to become your wife. But if you promise not to get cold feet and leave me suspended in anticipation another five years, I am willing to wait until Anna and Sun come back out here. But you must get them word immediately. It has already been too long as it is." Marybeth smiled at Isaac and poked his ribs with her finger. The two burst into laughter and childlike glee.

"Consider it done. And you need have no worry of my getting cold feet. I just hope you won't determine that you could do far better than marry an old man from the frontier and elect out of my simple but sincere proposal. I'll get a letter prepared and pass it along in hopes that it arrives in Boston within the year. And have I told you today that I love you, Marybeth?"

"You have. But you are welcome to do so at any time. And I love you Isaac Walker. I will be honored to become your wife."

*****

On the same day Marybeth and Isaac were talking about their upcoming marriage, the Continental Congress appointed George Washington Commander-in-Chief and issued bills of credit to fund the army in the sum of $2 million.

The following day, June 17, horrific fighting began at the Battle of Bunker Hill. An adjacent hill, later designated as Breed's Hill, saw the bulk of combat. Though the battle brought retreat of the American troops and gave the British control of Charlestown Peninsula, it was a pronounced morale boost for the Americans.

Chapter 7

Bunker Hill

"Gage made a big mistake when he abandoned this high ground." The young militia volunteer Hiram Ruston spoke with sincere conviction but held a hint of distaste in his voice. "And when Howe tries to come get us, we'll show him. They look really dandy gussied up in red coats and all, like they have never seen battle. But we'll show them, even if we don't look the part of proper soldiers." He and his companion William Clarkson turned their attention to tattered canvas knee breeches and black buckle shoes with the soles worn through.

"I would have to agree," Clarkson noted. "And it may seem they have been spared hardship. However, some of those men have made rigorous marches and faced more fire than we have."

"I suppose you're right, William. I guess there is just a modicum of jealousy in me when I consider their prim and proper ways and our rag-tag structure. We don't even have uniforms. But we are fighters. Wouldn't you agree, William?"

"That we are, my friend. Freedom is worth fighting for, and we have proven ourselves up to the challenge. Still, I wish there had been some way to avoid this wasteful war." William Clarkson became pensive.

"Avoid war? Why, we didn't bring this on. The King and his nonsense did that. We had not then nor have now any choice but to fight." Hiram Ruston spoke with conviction and youthful enthusiasm.

"Perhaps, but civilized people should be able to work out differences minus war, Hiram. Would it not have been more profitable for all involved to go to the table with negotiations, set greed aside and come up with a solution?"

"More profitable I suppose, but that King George is insufferable. William, you surely see that."

"As some of us here look at it, he is. But the way others see it, the King is simply doing what he should do. And that greed I mentioned. Seems it conquers all from time to time."

"That it does, William. That it does. And look at those Redcoats over there. I have to say those boys know how to move forward. Still, Howe must be shaking in his boots. Some of them can't be more than 300 yards from here. I think the two of us could take our long rifles, use a little elevation and make a few Redcoats keep their heads down."

"Yes, I'm sure we could, Hiram. These are some accurate weapons and we all know how to use them. But I have little interest in shooting at anyone, especially when I know my shot can go where I aim it and that it would account for another life."

"William, are you shirking your duty?"

"Hardly, but this conflict promises to be long and involved. I have heard and read a great deal of inspiring words, to be sure. But there is nothing pleasant about war. I want to get back to see my dear Rebecca. She and I parted on less than agreeable terms."

"You are in love, are you, William?"

"I am, and deeply. Rebecca needs me and I need her. I have little taste for war, but I feel it is necessary."

"But you, Rebecca and the children you will have deserve freedom."

"All people deserve freedom, Hiram. However, the only true freedom any of us will ever have is in a relationship with God. I doubt there will ever be lasting freedom and absence of war while we are in this human condition."

"Perhaps, but let's change the subject, William. There is something strangely uncomfortable about this line of conversation. What do you think of George Washington?"

"I think he is a great man. A man like all men in one regard, but a man of greatness just the same. He is dedicated to this experiment we are fighting for and has given up his all to see it through. Yes, a great man."

"Greater than those British leaders?"

"They, too, have a measure of greatness. British Generals and yes, Washington – all great men, men who have given all they have to the cause they believe in. We must not forget the efforts of great men. Some have proven formidable enemies and some stalwart allies. Greatness is present."

"But you mentioned God earlier. Don't you think He is on our side?"

"God has a greatness not known to nor possessed by man. And I believe He is on the side of all His people."

"Even the British, William? Is God on their side?"

"The British, the French, the Americans – all His people around the world. He has promised to never forsake His people."

"But how can He be on the side of those who are enemies?"

"I can't answer that. It just seems that war is most often an instrument of man, not of God."

"Well, I have never heard such outrageous talk, William Clarkson. Don't I hear you praying for your safety and the safety of your family?"

"You do, and often. Yes, I pray for my safety and the safety of my family, and for your safety as well, Hiram. I pray that God will deliver us from this. But I'm not sure praying for my safety at the expense of someone else is what God expects of me. And don't you think there are others on the opposing side who are praying for their safety as well?"

A thunderous rumble came from down-slope; a cannonball whistled its poisonous hiss over the redoubt. Hiram Rushton's life spilled onto the soil of Breed's Hill.

Chapter 8

Bain House

"Jonathan, Robert; please, come in." Jackson Bain offered a handshake to his brothers-in-law. "Thank you for coming. We have business to discuss, and it appears that we must view our future through the fog of war." All three were downcast. An eerie and haunting hush permeated the Bain House. Boston was in chaos.

"But even in the face of pronounced unrest, all is not drear." Jackson smiled at Robert. "Congratulations again to you and Cora. That was joyous news Mother proclaimed at the gathering last week. Another child - a blessing from God."

"That it is, Jackson, and thank you for reminding me." Robert Jamison could hardly contain himself. "Now what about you and Anna? And for that matter, Jonathan, what about you and Cassie? "

"Slow down, Robert. Anna and I have hardly had time to get acquainted. Patience. Children will come in time." Jackson smiled.

"Acquainted? That glow on Anna's face and bounce in your step tell me you are far more than just getting acquainted!" Robert turned a side-way glance at Jonathan and nodded toward Jackson. "We have you figured out."

"That we do." Jonathan broke his practiced protocol and entered a conversation that held no cause or opportunity for complaint or contempt. He, for the first time in Jackson's memory, was involved as an amiable participant. And for the first time in a long time, Jonathan was smiling. "Robert and I have been there. We know. Robert, one thing is sure."

"And what is that one thing, Jonathan?"

"It is sure that we are in the presence of a man who has made a most significant and powerful discovery!" Jonathan and Robert burst into roaring laughter that was entirely unlike them. In unison they pointed at Jackson as they rocked back and forth in jubilance. Jackson could not avoid the circumstances; he was the object of their merriment. He blushed uncontrollably.

"Gentlemen; gentlemen! Please. We have business matters to discuss." Jackson's attempt to restore some prescribed order was weak and unsuccessful.

"Well you certainly have business matters." Was it Robert or Jonathan's voice that proffered those words? Jackson was uncertain. Prospects were now hopeless. This was time only for laughter and at his expense. Business would have to wait.

*****

Frontier Settlement

"I hope that letter I sent to Boston arrived in a timely manner." Isaac looked at Marybeth with tenderness.

"And I hope the same." Marybeth Wallace embraced Isaac Walker, her love for him spilling from her eyes and smile. "When do you think Anna and Jackson will get the letter?"

"Oh, that is impossible to say. I simply got it on its way and prayed for a speedy delivery. I truly believe it has arrived already, that Anna and Jackson are now planning their return for the wedding. I did, however, tell Anna and Jackson that our schedule would depend on theirs. I encouraged them not to rush, to take all the time they need. I said we would wait until their return and then have the wedding."

"You are always kind, Isaac, and I appreciate your thinking of them and not wanting in any way to impose. Still, I'm not sure I can wait much longer. You have my head spinning with wonderment. I mean, what's a woman to do? With one such as Isaac Walker waiting to become her husband, a woman gets eager and giddy and full of anticipation. You are too good to miss!" Marybeth flirted and smiled like a teen.

"Goodness, Marybeth. Your opinion of me is greatly exaggerated, but I do thank you. Goodness!"

"Not exaggerated at all, Isaac. You are the man I love. But I can wait. Don't you worry about that. I was only teasing. Yes, I was being truthful, but we must accommodate Anna and Jackson. Their journey back here is not a simple thing. I respect you for considering them and I respect them as well. So, we must wait. That day will come and we will be married. Thank you, Isaac. I love you."

Chapter 9

The Frontier

"Liam Sullivan, are you going to force me to chase you all the way to Baltimore after all?" Lizza McDougall was jovial, teasing, flaming red hair accentuating passionate and mischievous eyes. "My, my. What must a girl do with a handsome man such as you?"

"What are you talking about, Lizza? Chasing me to Baltimore? I'm not going to Baltimore."

"Well, I can't be so sure of that. You ride out here to see me and then go back to the settlement to tend your flock. And then we drive the wagon to the settlement to attend church and hear your powerful sermons, but you never make a move past that. Are you running away to Baltimore?"

"Baltimore? No. What is this all about? I'm not going anywhere."

"Oh, it is just a comment I made to Anna some time back. I told her I would chase you to Baltimore if the need arose. I surely hope I don't have to do that."

"Chase me? Goodness; and I thought I was the one chasing you."

"Perhaps, but I'm ready to be caught and your chase just creeps along. Let's see; let me think a moment." Lizza twirled a strand of long, firey hair, pursed her lips and put two fingers to her chin. "It has been five months now and I don't recall your ever having kissed me. I could be wrong, but I surmise that a kiss from the strapping Reverend would be something I'd not forget." Reverend Sullivan blushed and looked downward as if he hoped the ground would swallow him and relieve his angst.

"Lizza, uh…."

"Yes."

"Such talk. And to your Pastor no less. What am I to make of you?"

"Make of me what you like, Liam."

"But I…. We…. Uh…."

"Speechless, are you? I would think by now you would be totally comfortable with me. I have made my feelings for you no secret. And as I recall, you asked permission to court me, which you obtained with ease. Now what?" Lizza paused and smiled as she watched Liam fret. "Oh, the Reverend Sullivan is abashed. Poor dear. Afraid of a little thing such as I." Lizza's toying with Liam was without restraint.

"Kiss you?"

"Yes, you may."

"No, Lizza; I was not asking. I was simply…."

"There is little need to ask. You have my permission."

"But I was just going to…."

"To kiss me? Well, I must say I have waited long enough for you to do so."

"But what would my congregation think?"

"What kind of question is that, Liam? Your congregation? They are all people, the same as you and I. What should they think? Goodness, Liam. Keep in mind that I am a member of your congregation, and I think kissing me is the perfect thing to do at a moment like this. Where is your spirit of adventure and romance?"

"It is here, Lizza. Right here with us right now". The one step each that separated the two was accomplished simultaneously. Liam held Lizza close and kissed her. A summer breeze drifting across the frontier landscape carried more than its customary promise.

*****

Boston

"Sun, you are not going to believe this." The letter had arrived sooner than Isaac had anticipated. Anna was ecstatic. Her eyes danced with animation and the smile seemed a permanent fixture across her beautiful face. "We got a letter from Isaac. You are not going to believe it." She handed the crumpled paper to Sun, and as he read, Anna watched his face brighten with every word.

"Isaac and Marybeth? Anna, this is wonderful news. Can you believe this? Isaac and Marybeth. The grandest announcement I have heard in a long time. Wonderful!"

"It is wonderful, my love. Wonderful, indeed." Anna rushed into Sun's arms and allowed him to twirl her about the parlor of Bain House. "Yes, it is wonderful. I can hardly wait to get back there and celebrate with them. What a pleasant and fulfilling surprise. Isaac is getting married."

"It is and we must. I wonder if Simon knows."

"If he doesn't, he will as quickly as we pass through the Yadkin. He and Nora Jean will want to share this with us. But knowing Simon, I suspect he has the ability to sense good news such as this. An amazing man, Simon Keats."

"He is that, Anna. I owe him a great deal. In fact, if it weren't for

Simon I may never have met you. Yes, my debt to that stubborn old coot can never be paid." Sun held Anna tightly. "I love you, Anna."

"And I you, Jackson. Can we leave by the end of the month?"

"Without question. We simply have to get back out there. Yes; by the end of the month. Let's begin making plans for the trip."

Anna's joy was suddenly sabotaged. The tears that began flowing were from a source she did not fully recognize. Were these the tears of joy from the delightful news she had just received? No. They were tears coming from deep within, from an ache that she had not yet brought to the surface, at least not to the surface with Sun. Foolish; she attempted to dismiss them. But that ache, those tears were relentless, pouring from her very core.

"Anna; dear Anna. What?" Sun's voice exhibited the same measure of pain as he saw in her eyes. He gathered her in his arms and allowed her sobs to come without shame. "Cry if you feel the need." Her heart seemed broken.

"It is all this good news I suppose." Anna still held the full truth tightly within. Marybeth and Isaac; Cora and Robert. A wedding; a baby." Anna was unable to say more at the moment.

"All joyous occasions I would say." Sun smiled.

"Yes, joyous." Anna brushed a tear from her cheek. "I'm pleased. It's just that I thought by now you and I…."

"Oh Anna. Please don't fret. Our child, our children, will come in God's good plan. It sounds empty that I ask you to give this time, but I don't intend it that way. I intend it as support, as a matter of faith. God is in control; He will sustain us through this and all other difficult and confusing elements of life. I love you." Sun held her. Tears were still present.

*****

"Come in." Jackson Bain sat behind an oak desk at Bain Enterprises and responded to the knock. Robert Jamison and Jonathan Richardson entered. They took seats in two oversized leather-covered chairs.

"Robert, how is Cora?" Sun showed genuine concern for his sister.

"Oh, fine, and thank you for asking. We can see evidence of our baby growing in her daily. Yes, she is fine. God has blessed."

"That He has. And Jonathan, what about Cassie? Is she well?"

"Doing well. She is pleased that you and Anna are here."

"And the children?"

"Yes, well. Growing like weeds." Jonathan smiled at the mention of his children.

"Gentlemen, we have business to discuss." Sun moved hastily to the purpose of this meeting. "We attempted it once before, but you two persisted in making me the brunt of your jokes and very little if anything was accomplished."

"Oh, I disagree, Jackson." Jonathan Richardson would not let the matter rest. "We firmly established that Anna has you…."

"Jonathan." Sun attempted firmness but could not hide the smile that began to grow.

"Yes, Jonathan and I discovered that Anna…."

"You too, Robert? Do I have no allies in my own brothers-in-law? Seriously now. We have business."

"We are serious, Sun." Jonathan could not avoid one last maneuver at Jackson's expense. "We are serious that Anna has put you under some powerful spell and that you are basically useless as regarding all matters save those of the heart. And other parts I suppose!" Boisterous laughter erupted from the trio. Business would have to wait for composure to once again take control. Jackson finally spoke.

"Are you two quite finished with your nonsense?" Sun wiped his eyes and the corners of his mouth.

"Not finished, but we can set it aside until another occasion." Robert still persisted.

"Very well. May we continue?"

"Indeed. Are you in agreement, Robert?" Jonathan Richardson was a man who had changed for the better. Robert nodded in the affirmative.

"First, I must advise you that Anna and I will leave late-month for a trip back to the frontier. We received notice that Isaac has proposed to Marybeth Wallace and the two will be married as quickly as we return."

"Another man about to be swept away into the abyss of power...."

"Jonathan!" Sun smiled but left the impression that he would not be led back into frivolity.

"Yes, sorry. Carry on."

"I just want to advise you two of our plans and will discuss this with Mother tonight. Anna and I will return as quickly as possible. Now to another matter before us. Turmoil reigns in our midst. War is a reality, and I fully expect the King to issue sanctions, perhaps even shut down commerce to the fullest extent of his ability until this conflict has ended. That said, it would be foolish for us to attempt any expansion and particularly foolish to attempt a launch of the freight business we discussed some time back. I feel that prudence leads us only in one direction, and that is to do our best to survive and keep Bain Enterprises stable until this matter is settled. What are your feelings on this?"

"Sadly, I agree." Robert Jamison was the first to speak. "I want this freight line badly, but a foolish investment of time and funds is hardly the way to begin. Yes, we must wait. And we must do our best to see that what we now have doesn't become insolvent. There is certainly no way to know what this war will bring. My vote is for cautious patience with hopes for a brighter future."

"I concur." Jonathan was somber but strong in his dedication and resolve. "We must take great care to protect what we have; our families and employees depend upon us to do just that. A tragic situation, but this could be for the best. We need to be free of the King's dictates. My hope and my expectation is that this country will emerge more vibrant than ever. You have my support."

"Thank you both. We shall do our best and keep a watchful eye on everything around us. It is my prayer that we can maintain some stability and continue to provide for our families and those in our employment. We have a great responsibility. Now with your permission, we will adjourn. We all have work waiting."

"And you must get back home to Anna so that…."

"Enough, Jonathan!" Handshakes accompanied laughter as the three parted.

Chapter 10

Boston

William Clarkson, now well acquainted with war scurried about the streets. He was under the command of Commander-in-Chief Washington. Rumors had begun to surface that a group of men would go to Fort Ticonderoga for the purpose of transporting cannon back to Boston. Clarkson intended to be among that group.

"William; William." Rebecca Bomar, having encountered William only briefly since her demands that he not enlist, ran to his side. She embraced him, sobbing as she did so. His long rifle, shot pouch, haversack, canteen and rolled-up blanket impeded his desired return of that embrace, making it less enthusiastic than he preferred. "I have missed you."

"And I you, Rebecca. You are the light of my life. I miss you every minute of every day. And I love you Rebecca."

"I love you, William. And I must apologize for my behavior that day in the parlor. All I could think of then was what I wanted and needed; I feared loss. But William, I was wrong. Can you forgive me?"

"Of course, but you owe me no apology. I understood then and I understand now. Like you, I was afraid. Still am – filled with fear but also resolve."

"But I didn't understand then. I could think of nothing but losing you and that was selfish. But now, I do understand. The fear is still there, but I am at peace – as much as that is possible I suppose. I admire you and realize that you were then and are now right regarding this struggle. We must break from the Mother Country and establish a government designed by and for the residents of this New Country, this under the leadership of God. I love you, William Clarkson. You take care of yourself and come back to me. That is an order."

"Yes mam. And I love you, Rebecca Bomar. Coming home to you as quickly as possible after all this is settled will be the driving force in my fight for liberty. Now I must hurry along to join the others. Good day, my love"

"And to you." Rebecca watched through tears as William disappeared. She walked away toward Bomar Mercantile.

*****

"We have to leave in short order, Anna." Jackson had a wagon packed and saddle horses tied behind. "If we don't get there soon, Isaac and Marybeth will get married without us." Anna acknowledged Sun and completed her farewells to the family.

"Yes, we really should go. Martha, take care of everyone while we are away. Sun and I will be back here as quickly as possible. I would like to think before Christmas, but that is not likely. I love you, and give my love to the others. Sun and I will be fine." Anna stepped into the July air and boarded a wagon outside Bain House. All waved their goodbyes as Anna and Jackson set off on an exciting but frightful journey of the unknown. British troops encircled Boston.

*****

"I implore you to halt progress and abandon your wagon immediately." A British officer stood in the roadway little more than an hour's travel from Bain House, his Brown Bess at port. "You would be well advised to follow instructions fully and with haste." Anna's face became ashen.

"Not again, Sun." She felt a dread that had not plagued her during that earlier stop as they neared Boston. "I am afraid."

"Please don't worry, Anna. Let's try to determine what this is all about." Sun also showed an increased concern, hesitant to speak quickly. "What is the meaning of this, Sir?"

"It, Sir, is not your place to question an officer of the King. It is I who will ask the questions and give the commands. Now if you will please, Sir, abandon that wagon." This one was not the officer from the trip into Boston. This one was different, gruff and more demanding. Perhaps even sinister, portentous.

"But we…." The officer transitioned his Brown Bess precariously toward Anna and Jackson. Others joined him.

"Please, if you will, direct those muskets otherwise." Sun tied the reins to the hitch in front of the wagon seat and helped Anna down. "We shall, if even under protest, oblige your commands." The two stepped to the ground. "Please explain this rude intrusion on our privacy."

"There is no privacy afforded you rebellious lot, nor do I owe you an explanation. No one is allowed into or out of Boston, Sir." The officer was curt. "Now you explain your intent and blatant disregard for British rule in this matter."

"Sir, if you will, we are going to the frontier to attend the wedding of my wife's father, a widower. We have no intent past that. Now if you will please excuse us and allow us to be on our way."

"I shall not. You must either return to Boston or be held as prisoners of the Crown."

"That, Sir, is absurd. We shall do neither. We shall only board this wagon and be…."

"Silence! I shall endure no insubordination from you or any other rebel force of this deranged and inconsequential movement that has created such undue inconvenience for the King. You speak only with my permission and in response to my queries. Now I presume that wagon carries supplies and munitions for troops ensconced in the hills there. You shall be truthful in your answer."

"There are no supplies other than our personal belongings." Sun was forceful but spoke with respect. "And as for munitions or other supplies suitable for a military effort, nothing remains in Boston of any import to such efforts. Conditions there are becoming dire. I have only my York rifle, one pistol, some few clothes and a brief food supply."

"'Tis uplifting to learn that conditions are dire in Boston." A quiet stir arose among the British, with low snickers erupting before the officer sent his scowl toward the troops around him. "Now please move away from the wagon and take your station there under that tree." The officer pointed to the side of the road and enlisted two guards to accompany Anna and Jackson.

Within minutes a flurry of activity erupted in the wagon. Horses snorted and stamped. Anna stood trembling, tears flowing freely as she watched British troops fondle and scatter her most personal items of clothing. Sun held her, embarrassed for her and abashed that he had no power over this unnerving obtrusion upon dignity.

And thoughts again, like before; but these thoughts more painful, more desolate, more afflicting: *This one is a bad man; worse. A bad man or a good man? Does he love his wife, hold her gently when she cries, lie beside her with passion burning in both them and binding them as one, escort her proudly and with respect? Does he ignore her, speak brashly, think he should never have married her? Good man or bad man? Does he coddle his children? Ride them on his back, dance with his young daughter perched on the tops of his feet?*

And does he have a son, perhaps old enough to accompany him while riding to the hounds? Does he shame that son, lecture and cajole? Does he treat that son with dignity? His father, Sun's father, told his mother, Sun's mother, that he, Sun's father, had no son. Debilitating to Sun. This thought shocked him, brought him around. How long had he been in this state of mesmerizing agony? Seconds; years? Not long, and then he was back there beside the tree, guards watching him watch the debauchery unfolding before him. Watching him watch his wife sob and blush and cover her eyes in shame.

"Nothing but beans and petticoats – and that handsome York rifle. A .54, is it?" The officer seemed to take delight in annoyance. Sun remained silent. "I see that you are ill prepared for military conflict. The only conflict I predict in your future is that you experience in your bedroom." Additional snickers, but these more pronounced than before. And the officer didn't reprimand his troops this time. Sun hung his head. "So, what are we to do with you two?"

"If I may speak, Sir." Sun was irate but remained in control of his emotions. He was also mortified, as a child who had been scolded away from the dinner table.

"You may."

"Please, Sir; we want nothing more than to go to the frontier and attend Isaac and Marybeth's wedding. We have no troop supplies as you have seen, and we are on no mission to deliver intelligence to military personnel. We simply desire a safe trip to visit family."

"As you say; as you say. We shall see. Now, tidy up that wagon. Clothes strewn about the ground is a dismal sight. And post haste, board that wagon and be on your way. I shall set troops beside you to assure your passage is to the frontier and not to some clandestine gathering of those intent upon furthering this useless cause you rebels term revolution." The officer designated an escort.

For the next two days there was little talk, the predominant sounds coming from rhythmic foot and hoof falls, rumbling wagon wheels and squeaking harness. But even minus conversation, Anna and Sun knew what was foremost in the other's mind. Freedom from the Mother Country and tyrannical government was a necessity.

*****

"You must think me a coward." The troops had left and Sun finally broached a painful subject. "I was powerless; I could not protect you. I am sorry, Anna."

"No, Sun; no. You were anything but powerless. You did protect me. That situation outside Boston was potentially hopeless. Your demeanor and wisdom were the power you needed. These resulted in my full protection. A coward? Never, never. You are my hero. Please, put such uncomforting thoughts out of your mind. You saved me from harm." Anna leaned close and kissed Sun. Two strong draft horses towed the wagon and its load closer to the frontier.

Chapter 11

Frontier – Early August 1775

Lizza McDougal was even more than her normally jubilant, vivacious self. She was perfectly giddy. Late-summer mornings had increased her energy and added a pronounced bounce to her step, making her a pure bundle of enthusiasm.

"He's coming, Papa." Lizza could not contain herself. She had just moments earlier unfurled and brushed her long red hair so that it flowed in sensuous ringlets down white shoulders and neck. A newly washed dress clung closely enough to her torso to make it near provocative yet reasonably modest. "Liam is coming today. And with all this talk of Isaac and Marybeth's engagement, I hope it puts a spirit of pursuit in Liam. What if he proposes marriage to me today, Papa?"

"Goodness, girl. You best run down there to the creek and cool off." Oscar partially chided but deep within was pained that he must concede his daughter was now a woman. "Could you be rushing things a little? You have known the Reverend Sullivan less than a year. Is that enough time?"

"Oh, more than enough. He is the man of my dreams. I love

him, Papa. And I know he loves me."

"Has he told you that, Lizza?"

"Well, not exactly. But I know he is in love with me as well. I want to marry him, to bear his children, to be by his side as he ministers to the church and community. No question, I am in love."

"I can well see that, but do you love Reverend Sullivan? Being in love and loving can often be different. In love may come and go to some degree, but love remains." Oscar was uncomfortable with the conversation but knew he must address these matters.

"Oh, Papa; I know that. I haven't experienced years as you have, but I know – at least in my head – about love. Not so solid sure about my heart, though. It probably rules at this time. Papa, you and Mama have raised me well. I've seen love lived out through you two. I know Jesus as my Lord and I love Liam. You should have no worries about this."

"Perhaps, Lizza. But I am your father and you my little girl – now all grown up. You must indulge me in this for a while."

"I will; I understand a little about your concern. Papa, I know we can do something for the first time only once. That truth tends to cloud judgement through anticipation and excitement. We don't know, so we look forward to the experience and can hardly wait. Then life takes hold. Excitement is no longer as exciting. But please realize that I have given this thought for some time now and have, to the best of my ability, come to terms with it. The love I have for Liam and the faith I have in God are sufficient to ride out the storms of life. Please don't worry that I have not given thought to anything past a wedding night."

"Oh, I do know that, Lizza. I trust you, I trust Reverend Sullivan and most of all I trust God. When the time comes, you will have my blessing. Can't speak for Matilda, though. She is your mother, and mothers are sometimes strange creatures. I simply can't image life without Matilda and am sure you feel that way about Liam. I'm sorry, Reverend Sullivan. Not accustomed to calling him by his first name; that's not how I was raised."

"You best get accustomed to it, Papa. Your son-in-law will be Liam Sullivan, and he just happens to be a Reverend. I intend to marry him, even if he doesn't recognize that fact yet! Thank you, Papa. I love you."

*****

Frontier Settlement

"Where do you want to have our wedding, Marybeth? I'm guessing the church here in the settlement."

"Yes, please. I think that only proper, Isaac. The church is where you and I met, and our closest friends attend there. I would like to marry in the church. And Reverend Sullivan will perform the ceremony."

"Of course. That is how it should be. And maybe Anna and Jackson have a part?"

"Without question. Anna will be my maid of honor and Jackson can be your best man. That would be perfect. What do you think?"

"Perfect, Marybeth. Oh, and Simon can sing a solo. His pitch won't be exactly right and he may screech more than sing, but it will be a joyous explosion of sound that will be heard all the way to the Cumberland. What do you think of that?" Isaac teased Marybeth.

"Well, let's not get carried away here, Isaac. I want a dignified wedding, not a long-hunter festival more suited for the Middle Ground. Really; Simon and a solo?"

"No, not really, Marybeth." Isaac smiled. "But then again, it would add a certain uncommon cultural flavor to the festivities."

"That is true. A cultural flavor that would have the panthers screaming and wolves howling. Buggy horses would tear loose from their hitching posts and run amuck toward the mountains. Dogs would seek refuge under porches. Little children would scuttle behind their mothers' skirts. I want Simon present but not heard – at least not heard singing a solo. He will definitely be heard, and there is nothing we can do to change that. But I wouldn't want to change that. So no solo from Simon. Agreed?"

"Agreed," Mayrbeth.

Chapter 12

Eastern Frontier – Late August 1775

July 5, 1775, Congress had endorsed the Olive-Branch Petition, a proposal for the recognition of American rights and an end to the Intolerable Acts. If this were done, a cease fire would be called. But George III would not agree. As a result, on August 23 the colonies were declared in open rebellion.

*****

"Please, Lord; not again." Anna recoiled on the wagon seat and grabbed Sun's arm. "Look; over there. Are those riders more British soldiers coming to harass us? Please; no, no."

"Not this far west." Sun stopped the team to get a better look at the hillside 200 yards off. "They are not wearing British uniforms. They look more like long hunters. But even that is not likely. I fear they are a band of marauders. Quick; slide back into the wagon and take whatever cover is available." Sun stepped from the seat and grabbed his York rifle. He laid the pistol in easy reach and checked its prime.

A beautiful, tranquil summer day, and now this. Evil; disruption; disrespect. Sun let troubling thoughts flit through his mind, thoughts somehow suggesting that God was absent or at least distant in this world he had experienced of late. *War; greed; hate.* Though he knew God was always present and caring, Sun wanted to rave and shout. Wanted to be angry. But angry at whom? He clinched his fists and dared a glimpse skyward, his entire being knotted and strangled and tortured.

"Well, well; what we done found here? Lookie boys. 'Ppears we done caught us a right-smart gentleman. And we seen that little woman what crawled back there to hide." The talker, Sun assumed, was an unofficial leader of this untoward collection of renegades. "What side you a' fightin' for there dandy, British or 'Mericans?"

"I conclude that Colonists should break from the Mother Country and form their own government, but I haven't yet taken up arms." Sun spoke firmly, but a hint of fear dampened his voice. Anna's wellbeing was gravely threatened by a group such as this. They had no allegiance apart from that they gave to themselves, and they certainly did not conform to any law. This situation was massively dangerous, and Sun was virtually powerless in the matter.

"Did you hear them gentleman words there boys? 'I conclude that Colonists….'" A gruff laugh erupted from an abominable mouth, revealing stained teeth that lay behind whisker stubble. "And while you a' bein' all gentleman like and talkin' them fancy words, maybe you oughta' move kinda slow like and put that big flinter you holdin' back in the wagen. And don't even give thought to grabbin' that there pistol." Sun obliged, his mind consumed by the fear that Anna would be harmed.

"What do you lads want from us?" Sun was poised but overwhelmed by anxiety, disgust so thick that it would surely drip from his face like summer sweat. "We have nothing to offer. There are only a very few supplies in this wagon, and we are simply going to the frontier to visit family. No ill intent is meant for anyone, so if you will kindly let us pass we will be grateful."

"Nothin' to offer, he says. Did you hear that there boys? Or lads he called us. He just don't think he ain't got nothin' to offer. Looks like to me he's got a whole bunch of offerins' right up there somewhur in that there wagen. And whur is that little woman; stuck under that there piece of canvas?" Anna's heart raced at his boisterous and profane words. "Come on outta' there little lady and let us lads have a look see."

"Please, don't bother her. She is my wife, innocent and trustworthy, a true woman of God. She affords no harm and asks only to travel in safety. I plead with you. Leave her undisturbed." Sun was shaken.

"Oh now, we just want a little look see." One of the ruffians threw back the canvas and grabbed Anna's arm, issuing her from the fragile cocoon.

"Leave her alone," Sun shouted. His entire body now rigid, fear mixed with infuriation. One step forward was met by a jab from the muzzle of a long rifle which made contact just above Sun's waist sash. His breath rushed out and he dropped to his knees. One member of the party snatched Anna from the wagon, grabbed the top of her dress and gave a great tug that ripped the outer garment away, leaving only the thin petticoat as a covering. She screamed.

Sun rose with all the haste he could garner in this breathless state. He rushed the culprit who had mistreated Anna, but the walnut butt of an English fowling piece against his left cheek and ear stopped all progress. Sun collapsed, unconscious.

*****

An hour later Sun's senses were still numb. He tried to focus his eyes, but the ground below and sky above were spinning. He managed a weak brush of his left hand to that battered cheek and grimaced. Anna sat nearby, head down, hair undone, a frightened stare directed toward nothing or no one. She clasped a tattered dress to her chest. "Anna." Sun's attempt at speech was weak.

"Anna, where are you?" No answer came, but Anna managed to slide closer, only enough strength remaining in her resolve to place herself alongside her husband, her body trembling with near-silent and tortured whimpers.

Chapter 13

Frontier

"My, my; a handsome horse and a more handsome rider I must say." Lizza McDougall had not done as her father advised and gone to the creek to cool off. She had instead fretted with her hair and paced around the yard in anticipation of Reverend Liam Sullivan's arrival. "Please step down Reverend and come onto the porch." Liam obliged.

"Lizza, good day." Liam tipped his hat. "You look stunning." She twirled a strand of her flashing red hair.

"Thank you kindly, Reverend." Lizza attempted demureness, but her passionate spirit impeded such action. "I try to look presentable when company comes, so I quickly ran a brush through my hair and put on this simple little dress. It is rather old, nothing special."

"Perhaps, but if that is nothing special and if that is simplicity, I have never seen those two elements more flattering. You are radiant, Lizza. Truly radiant."

"Liam Sullivan; now that is more like it. Does this late summer air have you soaring to new heights? Have your thoughts recently been on matters other than the congregation? Indeed, more like it."

"I suppose I could answer yes to both those questions. The

weather is grand, I have thought a great deal about you of late and I feel more alive than ever. Did I tell you that you are radiant?"

"You did, and feel free to do so any time. Now, aren't you going to gather me in your arms and smother me with kisses?"

"Lizza, goodness no. Your parents – Matilda and Oscar. And the children. What will they say?"

"I won't tell them if you won't."

"But they will see us."

"Not if we go hide."

"Lizza."

"Don't Lizzza me, Liam Sullivan. I can't wait. Now, come on." Lizza grabbed Liam's hand and led him around the corner of the house. Their brief time there was one of whirling emotions and spontaneity. Presently they returned to the porch and sat on a pine bench.

"Goodness, Lizza. Goodness." Liam wiped his forehead with a kerchief.

"Yes, goodness." Lizza's heart was racing.

"I am sure you are aware of Isaac and Marybeth's impending marriage." Liam finally found breath to speak.

"I am. Seems that word has spread widely. I hope Anna and Sun can come back for the ceremony."

"As I understand it, Isaac sent a letter and fully expects them to be here by early September. He and Marybeth plan to wait until Anna and Sun return. I do hope, as I am sure you do, to see them ride up any day now. The sooner the better in Marybeth and Isaac's eyes. Those two are in love."

"Oh, they surely are. And it is so very romantic. Have you ever been in love, Liam?"

"I thought I was once."

"With Anna?"

"Well, I must admit. Yes, with Anna. There was a fondness and genuine concern and respect, but I was not in love. Anna kept talking about a glow. I thought it foolish at the time, was even condescending toward Anna regarding that matter. But she was right. There should be…, no, must be a glow."

"And now, Liam?"

"Glowing brighter than a barn lantern!" The two laughed wildly. Lizza was seeing Reverend Sullivan in a way she had not seen him before.

"Me too – glowing." Lizza locked her fingers tightly with Liam's.

"I am truly excited for Marybeth and Isaac, Lizza. They are wonderful and deserving individuals, and God has seen fit to put them together. A grand union, I must say." Liam appeared fully caught up in matters of the heart.

"Oh, I agree. I can hardly wait to go to that wedding." Lizza virtually bubbled. "I hope you and I can dance all night after that celebration."

"Now easy, Lizza. All night? First, I will be extremely busy with the wedding, and I must attend to a number of duties surrounding the reception and festive gathering; I will be tired. And second, you have seen me dance!"

"I have, and you are a master. Light and graceful you are. I would very much like to dance with you all night. But if we were married we would have to find some time in the dancing to stop and…."

"What are you saying, Lizza? Goodness me. I am embarrassed."

"You best get over that, Liam. I did say if we were married. Why should you be embarrassed?"

"Oh, it's just that…."

"Just that what?"

"Oh, you know, Lizza."

"No, I'm not sure I do know."

"You do know – all this personal talk and the like. And I have never…."

"Nor have I, Liam. You are aware of that. But I am ready, that is ready when God puts us together in marriage." Lizza's countenance revealed contemplation.

"It seems marriage, in one form or the other, is the primary focus of conversation today." Liam loosed his grip on Lizza's hand and moved to face her directly. "Lizza, I have been thinking of late; thinking deeply. And I…."

"You what, Liam? Plesae continue."

"I shall. Please be patient." Liam's mouth was dry, his speech halted.

"Of course. I have never been one to rush in matters of the heart." Lizza's eyes darted, she twirled a strand of red hair and her lips formed an alluring and inviting smile.

"No, no; not Lizza McDougall. She is the reserved and shy one in such dealings."

"I am that. Now go on. You were saying?"

"I was just saying that with all this marriage business surrounding us and becoming the community talk, perhaps I should…."

"Oh, yes; you should. You definitely should." Lizza was ecstatic. "Lizza, I want to ask you…."

"Well hello, Reverend." Oscar McDougall threw open the cabin door and stepped onto the porch. "It is good to see you. We are pleased you have come to visit. Is Lizza entertaining you this morning?"

"She is that, Sir. And hello to you. She and I have been talking of…well, serious matters." Liam Sullivan searched for words.

"Yes, yes. Of course. A wedding I am sure." Oscar smiled. Lizza did the same as she twirled that strand of red hair. Liam Sullivan tucked his head and wanted to disappear.

"Uh, yes. But I haven't even…. Uh, I mean…. I need to talk

more with…."

"Marybeth and Isaac?" Oscar interrupted. "Just don't you worry. Those two are absolutely in love and ready for a wedding. And you don't have to be concerned; you'll do just fine.?"

Liam jerked to attention as Lizza howled in boisterous laughter at his angst. Or perhaps the laughter was because of the narrow escape from what she and obviously Liam thought was clearly the threshold of confession. "Yes, Sir. I have my books and instructions. They taught us how to do such things in divinity school." Lizza was out of control with mirth.

Chapter 14

Eastern Frontier

The night chill had not been sufficient to coax Anna and Sun from their poses of anguish. Daybreak found them still lying beside the wagon. Sun had occasionally been aware of Anna's shivering sighs but was helpless to comfort her. She, similarly, had heard soft moans from him but was also helpless. They had simply lain there, side by side and aching with individual and communal pain. Sun stirred.

"Anna." His voice was strained and weak. "Are you awake?"

"Yes." Just that one muffled word was enough to proclaim alarm.

"What has happened to us?" Sun attempted to sit up but had to abandon the struggle. A pain deep within his belly and a pounding head were victors of that first try. Anna remained silent – and still, apart from those bouts with shivering.

"Anna." Sun made another effort, this one more successful. He sat looking at her, crumpled and battered, only a fragment of her outer garments in place. He first touched her cheek and then her shoulder, both gently. "Can you talk; can you sit up?" Anna moaned, her eyes closed in a foiled effort to forget.

"Anna, we must get up. We need help." Sun managed to gain

footing and stood, wobbling, looking down at this precious gift that he never considered would be in a condition such as what he saw. He had promised to protect her from harm. But he hadn't. He couldn't.

"Please, Sun. I never want to get up again. Please, leave me."

"Never, Anna; never. I must get you in the wagon and find help. This is my fault. Or is it God's fault? I tried to protect you and couldn't. He could have and didn't." Sun's words were distant, unlike him. He would never say such things. He would never feel this way. But Anna knew it was Sun speaking and in her heart she was mimicking those same sentiments. Sun stretched, looked at his hands, and then knelt on one knee beside her. "Come; let me help you stand."

Though no visible signs of injury were present, Anna was frail, weak, as if she were in the midst of some dread disease. But that disease, they both recognized, was not physical. It was a sickness coming from a loss of security, from an attack on dignity and self-esteem, from humiliation. Sun brushed a tag of matted hair from her face. "Oh, Anna; my dear Anna."

*****

Boston

William Clarkson would for the remainder of his life be maimed. The ball from a British Brown Bess had impacted his left leg just below the knee. A crude procedure hardly deserving the designation medicine was employed to remove the dangling appendage at the point where that ball made contact. Though a quickly-fabricated pair of crutches with which he had barely had time to grow familiar made him mobile, he was not the physical specimen he had been.

"Rebecca." Clarkson stood on the porch of the Bomars' house when Rebecca opened the door. "Hello Rebecca." He hung his head.

"William. Oh dear William. I heard." Though Rebecca thought she was prepared for this meeting, she was still shocked. She tried not to stare. "How are you?" Rebecca was abashed by her own words. How could she proffer such a senseless, thoughtless question? How could she be so hesitant to reach out and hold him, the one thing she wanted most to do? How? "My sincere apologies, William. What a foolish response. Please forgive me."

"Other than this loss, I am fine. Just fine." William gestured to his leg, cynicism occupying his words, his expression, his very core. "A man with half of one leg missing is the perfect portrait of virility. Thank you for asking." He remained stoic, his gaze now fixed on Rebecca's face, but that gaze was appropriately blank. "Aren't you going to invite me in, or is it too unthinkable to take company with one who is suddenly not the same person he was at our last meeting? Shall I simply turn and walk away, that is, limp away and leave you to your disillusionment?"

Rebecca could not believe what she was hearing. The man who had pledged his love to her saying such things. The man whom she loved so harsh and bitter. The man she thought she knew, now a stranger. How could this be? Rebecca's face was ashen, tears flowing out of control. Her ability to even speak practically lost. She managed only to say, "Please come in."

*****

God had strengthened Anna and Sun, had blessed and allowed them to locate a small homestead occupied by a kind and gracious couple, both of whom were getting on in age. But Anna and Sun didn't seem to recognize His working. They were engulfed by anger and discouragement and shock. Neither had talked much during those days of getting to the homestead and their subsequent convalescence. They simply sat in blackness, despite the concern shown by their hosts. God, it seemed to Anna and Sun, was nowhere to be found.

"While I was unconscious, while I was there on the ground and unaware of my surroundings, what happened, Anna?" Sun had not asked for a detailed account prior to this but was a bit more talkative than he had been since they left the homestead the day before. The old man of the household had asked that God bless them on the remainder of their journey and invited them to stop by anytime. Sun had heard the man, but his words were inconsequential. Something akin to hate was seething in Sun's heart.

"They pushed and shoved me, tore my outer garments off. And then they just stood there looking and laughing and shouting among themselves." Anna found it near impossible to remember and voice the episode. "I cried to God for deliverance and kept telling those men that God loved them even in the midst of this evil."

"And where was God, Anna? Where was He?" Sun scowled and gripped the horses' reins in disgust. "Did He deliver you? Does He really love such trashy dogs as those? Tell me Anna. Tell me."

"God was.... I.... I...." Anna had no words. She, too, had been troubled and filled with questions.

"And I must ask. Forgive me, but I must. Anna, did they...?"

"No, Sun; no. I feared they would, but they simply stood there and mocked me."

"How, then, did it end? What did they do afterward? I could not have been out very long, and they were gone when I regained my senses. What?"

"They simply rode away. Sun, they just mounted their horses and rode away." Anna fell silent, her mind whirling and eyes showing a hint of light for the first time since the incident. "Sun, maybe God...."

"They will pay for this." Sun interrupted, his face resolute, flamed with anger. "They will pay. If I ever find any of those men, I will extract my revenge. I shall not wait for retribution to come from God or some other outside and distant force. I will tend to those men in a form that will bring immediate justice. They will pay." Anna was now crying – again. What was happening to them, she and Sun? Who was this man she loved? Who was she?

Chapter 15

The Frontier, Early September

"Good day, Reverend Sullivan." Oscar McDougall stepped from the porch and began to move toward the barn to begin his farm chores. "You two enjoy the morning, and Reverend, I shall see you soon."

"Thank you, Sir." Liam Sullivan exhaled a soft sigh that he and Lizza were again alone and had not aroused the curiosity of Oscar - or at least Liam hoped. "Can I help you in some way with the chores, Sir?"

"Not at all, Reverend. You two have far more important matters to discuss. So thank you, but you just enjoy the day and think about that fine sermon you will present Sunday." Oscar waved a brief fare-well as he entered the barn.

"Not a word, Lizza." Liam wagged his finger at her and smiled. "I know you and I - me in particular – were caught in an awkward situation on my last visit. Seems your father is always close by. I surely am glad he came outside that day while we were doing nothing but talking. A few minutes earlier and just around there would have been tragic." Liam nodded toward the corner of the house, the locale of their passionate kiss.

"Tragic?" Lizza attempted a pouting face, but her smile belied the posture. "Is that how you view my kisses – tragic?"

"Well of course not. I was just saying that it would have been tragic for Oscar to have caught us in such a compromising situation. I mean, I am his minister, your minister. What would he think…?"

"Liam, we have been there before." Lizza spoke firmly, but her care and understanding for Liam Sullivan was obvious. She was not teasing so much this time. "I understand your position on this and other matters. You are, after all, a pastor, the church's leader. Nothing untoward should be a part of your conduct. I do understand. But some day, maybe soon, we will be…."

"Yes we will." Liam Sullivan was fully assured and ready to move forward with this relationship. He knelt before Lizza McDougall and took her hands in his.

"Oh, Liam."

"Yes, Lizza. I love you. I have prayed about this decision for some time now and am convinced that God brought you into my life. I want you to be a part of that life, a part not in the same way as you and your family are already, but a more significant part. That part that can only be filled by a wife. So Lizza McDougall, will you marry me?"

"Yes, Liam Sullivan, I will marry you. Gladly, happily – I will marry you. I love you, Liam."

Liam stood, pulled Lizza to him and kissed her. "No tragedy there I'd say!"

"None at all." Lizza smiled and kissed him. "Now all that remains, other than the ceremony, is for you to ask permission of my papa. He's right there in the barn."

"Now, Lizza?"

"Well of course. What better time is there? You rush over there and get that done and we will soon be celebrating. Now off with you; he's right over there in the barn."

"As you say." Liam began his short but tortuous trip.

"And Reverend Liam Sullivan." Lizza could not avoid one last jest at his expense. "You are a fine pastor and preacher, but heed this warning. I will soon show you what preaching is all about!"

"Oh, Lizza; shush. Someone will hear you. Goodness, Lizza; goodness. What shall I do with you?" Both Liam and Lizza smiled.

*****

Boston

William Clarkson entered Bomar House, his struggle with the crutches not unnoticed by Rebecca. She directed him to the parlor, and he, unlike his customary action of the past, went to a single chair and sat. Even he was not sure if this decision was driven by the awkwardness of his mobility or some sinister ploy to remain separated as far as possible at the moment from Rebecca. The two of them always, in the past at least, chose a small sofa sized for a couple. He let his rude crutches thud to the floor.

"Well, Rebecca, here we are. The loving couple, the couple destined for marriage and a happy family and a robust career in the mercantile business. A house filled with active and adoring children. The perfect dream come to fruition. Here we are. And I regret that I have destroyed that dream, have turned it into a colossal nightmare. Sincere apologies, my dear." William was gruff, as if some hideous beast had overtaken him, had set up residence in his heart. And while Rebecca could not be certain, she still hoped that the William Clarkson she loved was yet hidden somewhere deep inside.

"Yes, William; here we are." Rebecca was crushed, confused,

perhaps even angry.

"And before you break into a tirade of 'I told you so,' allow me to say I had to do it. Wrong to do so, as it seems to have turned out, but I had to. I could not go on and face what I then thought would be our life together and not take a firm stand on what I concluded was best and right, not stand firm in defense of what I perceived this experiment of a new country should look like. I had to, and I brought only destruction to all involved, most of all to myself."

"And why would you expect me to 'break into a tirade' as you put it?" Rebecca was downcast. "We had this discussion earlier, after Bunker Hill. I told you I was wrong in my initial action, in my forbidding you to take up arms." Rebecca found it difficult to even say those words. She had done so, but she had also come to see William's point of view. "You know I came to support you in that decision."

"So you say. But that was before what you feared and questioned me about became reality. Now things are different. I am an instrument of destruction."

"An instrument of destruction? What could you possibly mean by that?"

"My choices destroyed your dreams, my dreams. Those dreams are now destroyed, and it was I who allowed that destruction; no, it was I who implemented it, who caused that destruction."

"It was this war, that huge lead projectile that cost you half your leg. But I fail to see how either or both the war or the projectile destroyed our dreams. And it certainly was not you."

"Just look at me and you will see how." William showed anger, a hurt that was far deeper than any physical wound. "Look at me and tell me what you see, Rebecca."

"I see the man I loved before he went to war, and I see the man I still love – though he is angry and fatigued and most certainly frightened. That's what I see. Perhaps you would prefer me to say I see a man I pity, a man who deserves sympathy and one who thinks others should celebrate his wallowing in self-doubt. I can see him as well, but I refuse to look at that man. I refuse to allow him the privilege of toying with my emotions and sharing his misplaced guilt. His refusal to accept what the past has given and move forward. That man I won't look at, won't abide." Rebecca fell silent.

"Oh, you do, do you?" William was curt and taken aback.

"I do and I will and I won't and all those other things I said." Rebecca stood firm on her proclamations."

"That is not what I expected when I came here."

"Did you expect me to simply sit quietly, to shake my head in agreement that all is lost? To allow you to transfer your self-centered-ness onto me and disrupt my dreams as you put it? To consider you my poor baby and allow you to drag the world down around you into doubt and frustration? If so, I refuse. I will cry with you when it is appropriate. I will suffer with and stand by you in all things, even this if it is viewed with reason. But I will not permit you to walk in here with some distorted view of reality and fabricated guilt and expect me to simply accept it without question."

"Well.... I can't really believe you...."

"William, you listen to me and do your best to hear what I am saying. I will say this only once as it relates to this present situation."

"I will listen."

"I love you, William. I have for a long time and I do now. You lost your leg, not your heart or your mental faculties or your support from my father, your employer, nor from your employees. You are creative, intelligent and highly productive in your endeavors. If you came here to tell me you no longer love me and that you are ending our relationship, so be it. I can accept that. But if you came here to, in a twisted sort of way, shame me, and yourself I might add, into a life of useless mourning and perhaps even depravity, I will not be a part of it. In fact, I will end the relationship and save you the bother. Contrary to what you say and how you feel, you have not lost all. Most importantly, you have not lost God. He is right there where you left him. Please, show yourself out. I have other matters to address. Good day, William"

Chapter 16

Near the Keats Cabin

"How do I face Simon?" Sun spoke softly, but anger still plagued him. Unlike himself, he slouched, his head low as if he were trying to hide. And he was trying to hide – hide the anger and hurt and frustration and shattered self-worth. How so many plagues could have consumed him in such a short time was beyond his ability to grasp. He dreaded seeing Simon, a sensation he had never felt when considering this man he loved and admired. "How do I face him?" Sun coaxed the horses forward, that leathery squeak of harness accompanying.

"I can't answer that, Sun." Anna was yet broken. She, as Sun, could think of little other than brutality, a spent spirit, mental suffering. "I can't answer because I can't determine how to face anyone at this time. I am shamed and heartsick, Sun. I feel that I may have lost myself."

"You have no reason to feel shame, Anna. None of that was your fault, and you certainly were not complicit in any of it. You were, you are, the victim."

"As are you, Sun. A victim. Not complicit. Not at fault." Anna attempted some measure of resolve.

"And though your heart is sick, and perhaps will be for some time to come, you certainly have not lost yourself. You are still the beautiful and loved Anna Walker Bain, my dear wife. It may be diffi-cult for you to see right now, but it is truth." Sun was gentle. However, that rage was still holding him captive.

"My dear Sun." Anna barely whispered. "Your words are poetic even in the face of tragedy. But your words or the words of anyone else can't soothe my burden completely. Only God can do that." Sun heard her, but his mind was unable to process anything related to God. He was focused on revenge. God was not a part of that. "And you, we, face Simon and Nora Jean and Isaac and all others with our heads held high and our hearts set on love." Anna hardly believed what she said. Sun shrugged. *Where was God; would He repair the damage, the distress?*

*****

Keats Cabin

"Nora Jean; ho, Nora Jean. Come on in here quick. Looky, looky. Down the ways a bit in that there wagon. Iffin my ole eyes ain't janking with me, that yonder is Miss Anna and the Boston youngster. Well bust my weskit and slap off my hat. That there is them; shorely is. Glad I'm all spiffied up and such like, for that there's some citified vis-tors a' comin'. Glory be. I'm ready to do some speachafyin'." Simon Keats roared in laughter as he slapped his leg and then gathered Nora Jean in a giant hug.

"Speachafyin'?" Simon Keats, what language are you speaking? And spiffied up? If you mean dressed properly for company, you are not too spiffy. That three-day beard just burned my cheek, and that weskit you mentioned bursting looks as if it just got back from a long hunt. But I must tell you that you are welcome to burn my cheek with your whiskers any time you want, and I love that old weskit – at least as long as you are wearing it. I love you. You old goat. And yes, that is Anna and Jackson. Rush on out there and greet them."

*****

"Well now, climb on down offin that there wagon and let your ole friend Simon give you youngsters a big ole frontier hug. Iffin you two ain't a pleasome sight. Yessireee, a shorely pleasemone sight. Git on down here and let's git a plumb proper like greetin' done. How you two doin'? My, but you look healthsome 'nough. Maybe a bit trail weary but healthsome." Simon took Anna's hand and helped her down. He tried to gather her in a crushing embrace, but Anna pulled away. Simon restrained himself.

"Simon Keats, you old sour goat. How are you?" Sun wished to be jovial but his demeanor spoke of pain. He stepped to Anna's side without so much as a handshake for Simon.

"Well hello there, Boy. Now 'fore you say a word, let me tell you I see some hurtin' goin' on inside there – inside both of you young-sters. Ain't much a way of greetin' somebody you ain't seen in a too-long time, but I 'spect it shorely is more important than any proper greetin' right now. And just remember that Simon Keats is just plumb full of smartsomes and he'll help you outta this tangle you done got in. And remember that ain't nobody, 'cept maybe Isaac and shorely the Good Lord, loves you more than ole Simon Keats. Shorely do love you."

"And we thank you, Simon." Sun hugged Simon. "We love you as well." As Sun spoke, Anna watched and nodded in agreement but remained silent. "Simon, this is a protracted story and we must have

80

ample time to discuss it." Sun was perfunctory. "Shall I tend to my team and then we can talk?"

"Yessiree, Jackson. Whatever you need to do is just plumb fine with me. Let's you and me git your gear unloaded and we'll go stable the team. I'll fetch Nora Jean to come out here and take good care of Miss Anna." Simon refrained from his usual laughter. "Nora Jean." Simon's voice echoed across the countryside. "Come on out here iffin you can and see to Miss Anna. She probably needs a woman's touch for shore."

"Goodness, Simon. You could wake the sleeping from here to the frontier. I thought you said you would go fetch Nora Jean. Instead, you howl out a charge fit for fighting men." Sun scolded but only in a halfhearted effort.

"Oh, that ain't no never mind. That Nora Jean, she just loves Simon Keats and knows that Simon Keats just shorely loves her and ain't gonna disrespect her never. And she loves you youngsters near 'bout as much as she loves me. She'll be right along directly. In fact, here she comes now. Lookie. See what I done told you." Simon began a boisterous laugh but stopped short when he thought better of it under the current conditions.

"Simon Keats; stop your bellowing. What have I told you about that?" Nora Jean smiled and walked toward them. She customarily would have pulled Anna close and given her a deep and warm embrace, but something in the way both Anna and Sun looked stopped her. "Come along, dear. Let's the two of us go inside. And Jackson, it is so very good to see you."

"And you, Nora Jean. I thank you."

*****

The account given by Anna and Sun occupied a half day. Sun

with Simon; Anna with Nora Jean; all four of them together at times. It was a painful journey for all involved. Nora Jean cried with Anna; Simon agonized with Sun. That matter of revenge was particularly troubling. "Careful with that revenge thing, Boy. You gotta know that the man what you angry at leads you 'round like a hungry puppy. It ain't you a' gittin' him back much as it is him a' gittin' just 'bout ever'thing you got left inside. He lets you torment and destroy your own self while he's just a struttin' 'round with no never mind for you. He don't care. Iffin he did, he wouldn't uh done them bad things in the first place. Seems he ain't the one you need to put in control of your life there, does it?"

And Anna's shame spoke loudly to Nora Jean. "Shame can be beneficial when we become ashamed of poor behaviors that lead to sin. But shame assigned to us by others is not. That is one of Satan's biggest lies. He shames us for our sins and convinces us that we are unworthy. But we know better. If we have genuinely confessed our sins and asked for forgiveness and have turned from those sins, God forgets them, wipes them away. So the devil lies when he tells us otherwise.

"He cripples us, makes us want to hide, to run away. We then do become less than what we are and should be – that is until we get it all sorted out with God. When we do, we can be that light on a hill that Jesus wants us to be."

"Yes; I believe that." Anna spoke softly, her eyes showing more insight with each word Nora Jean spoke.

"But you know these things, Anna. You simply need to be reminded. And an ordeal such as you survived can certainly cloud memory and logic and security, perhaps even cause us to forget some essential truths we already knew."

"Yes, of course." Anna was listening, absorbing. "And while it is far easier to say than to grasp, you were not at fault, Anna.

You deserve no shame. You were innocent. That may take a long time to become reality to you, but it will. With God's help, it will. Simon, Jackson, Isaac, Mary Beth – all of us support you; we care. You have a team beside you. God is the leader of that team."

"Nora Jean, there is another matter." Anna's eyes immediately overflowed, warm tears, but they chilled like a winter rain. "A baby. I…I can't…." Anna could no longer talk; sobs consumed her.

"Oh my dear. Dear, dear Anna." Nora Jean joined Anna with tears of her own. "This is more than you can bear alone." They sat silently.

Later, Anna and Nora Jean prayed. Then they cried. Then they smiled.

Chapter 17

The Frontier

Liam Sullivan approached Oscar McDougall tentatively. Oscar wielded a broad, wooden-tined pitchfork and was removing litter from a barn stall. Liam noted Oscar's expansive shoulders and sturdy back; these belied Oscar's gentle nature and graciousness.

"Yes, Reverend. Come on over and visit. But be careful; you will soil your shoes and dust your weskit in here." Oscar was pleasant, his face wearing the grime of toil and a boyish smile. "Have you ever cleaned a stall?"

"No, Sir. I can't say that I have." Liam fidgeted. "But I shall be happy to learn if I can be of any assistance to you."

"Not at all, Reverend. I can handle this easily enough. But I do appreciate the offer." Oscar's smile seemed to grow; a glint of mischief flickered in his eyes. "And I doubt you came in here to gain instruction on the finer points of farm life."

"No, I did not come with that purpose in mind. Still, I shall assist...."

"Don't even consider it. Perhaps we should just move outside and talk." Oscar set the big fork down and walked through the barn door. An early-autumn sun embraced the countryside. A maple tree on the hillside showed a hint of yellowing. Shadows leaned curiously and spoke of cooler days and harvest and making meat, a common term applied to fall hunts that would produce smoked and jerked venison. "Join me, Reverend." They stepped into the shade of an oak and sat on blocks that would soon yield a winter's supply of firewood.

"Mr. McDougall, Lizza and I have been talking." Liam was reticent, his voice quivering.

"And I would guess you two have been doing a little more than talking." Oscar looked askance, smiled, his eyes sparkling.

"Well, Sir. Yes…we…uh. We…." Liam's composure went missing.

"That's all right, Reverend. I was your age once. Matilda and I understand. Yessiree; we understand! I don't mean to chide. Just relax and say your piece."

"Yes, Sir. Lizza and I….Well, we want to…get married. I asked Lizza and she accepted and now I am asking you for your permission." Liam Sullivan sighed and felt a great burden lift from his shoulders, a curtain pull away from his heart, his angst escape and glide upward into the autumn sunlight. He had done it; he had opened himself and become not just Reverend Sullivan but Liam the man, the human, the one who was deeply in love with Oscar's daughter.

"Well now; there you go. You did it. And quite suitably I must say. Now we have a few things to discuss." Oscar sat erect and eyed Liam.

"Yes, I am sure we do. But if you don't mind, before we begin with questions, please allow me to speak." Liam was taken aback at his own boldness.

"Agreed. Please, carry on."

"I love Lizza. I want only the best for her. I will dedicate myself to her and be a good husband – and father to our children should God bless us with them. I want Lizza to be my partner here as I minister to these dear people in the settlement and beyond. I hope this answers your questions."

"Some of them, yes. But there are others."

"Others?" Liam swallowed hard.

"Yes."

"How many others?"

"I can't say for sure, Reverend. I admit that you did a fine job of explaining just now. I thank you."

"You are welcome, Sir. Now, what other questions?"

"Just one at the moment."

"Yes, Sir. Feel free to ask." Liam smiled.

"Lizza." Oscar sighed. "Now that girl is wound tighter than a honeysuckle vine on a sweetgum. That flaming red hair is, I am convinced, indicative of her inner self. She will be difficult to handle; she will wear you to a frazzle. Are you prepared to be worn to a frazzle?" Oscar erupted into laughter and jabbed a finger at Liam's shoulder. "Are you up to it?" More laughter.

Liam was speechless. How could he respond? What should he say to this banter, this awkwardness? The father of his wife-to-be teasing and goading him. What? Liam refrained from speaking and simply sat, head down and face flushed.

"Well, I…. Uh…." At least Liam was finally trying to speak. "Before I deal with that, may I ask you a question?"

"You may, Reverend. Feel free."

"After Lizza and I are married – if you give your consent for us to marry – what shall I call you?" Liam was embarrassed at his own question.

"Father or Dad or Oscar – anything but Mr. McDougall. And what shall I call you? After all, you are my pastor; you are Reverend

Sullivan."

"Liam or Son – anything but Reverend Sullivan, Oscar."

"Well then, Liam, you have my consent! Marry that girl. Have a wonderful life and many children. And do your best not to stay worn out all time." Oscar and Liam shared in the laughter.

*****

Boston

William Clarkson stumbled slightly on the steps at Bomar House, but he righted himself with much more fluency than in days past. The crutches were more familiar now; still, he hoped to get a pair more precisely built very soon. He stopped at the door and knocked; his wait was brief. Rebecca was expecting him.

"Hello, William." Rebecca was gracious but perfunctory. Her appearance was perfection - a ruffled dress that hugged her body, a broach dangling neatly from her neck and accentuating her feminine shapeliness. Ringlets of hair hung precisely as they should over her shoulders. William didn't fail to recognize. "How are you? And I ask that with no apologies this time." Rebecca was kind but measured.

"Hello, Rebecca. I am doing well. And I do mean that; I am well. Better, in fact, than I have been since that encounter with the musket ball. Thank you for asking. And Rebecca, you are beautiful." William smiled and nodded; a full bow was yet beyond him.

"Please, come in." Rebecca stepped aside and issued him into the house. "Come with me to the parlor."

"May I sit with you on the sofa?" William was apprehensive, but he did want to be close to Rebecca, a dramatic metamorphosis when compared to his last visit.

"As you wish, William." The two of them moved to the sofa.

William was awkward in taking a seat, but he was improving. He laid the crutches to his side gently. Rebecca and William sat – rigid and prescribed, a chasm still separating them. Not a chasm of physical distance but a chasm of emotional dysphoria.

"So, you really are doing well, William? I am praying for you in this matter."

"Thank you, and yes, I am doing well. This entire episode was one for which I was not prepared. I should have been; I am the one who chose to take up arms. Still, I was not prepared." William spoke calmly, with some degree of resolve.

"I am pleased and hope that you continue to heal. But you just made a statement that alarmed me, indicated to me that you are not yet in a proper mindset. That thing about you taking up arms and all it implies, I will not hear that. I assured you during that last visit that the subject was not now nor would it become an issue. I refuse to become a victim, will not serve as your accomplice in self-pity. I care too much to do so." Rebecca fell silent.

"Oh; no please, Rebecca. I don't intend to do that or go there in that same cloud of anger and disgust as I had earlier. I should never have mentioned it today, and I can't now promise to never mention it again. It is just still too real to put it completely out of my mind. But I am healing, better, much improved from that previous state that strangled me during the last visit. My apologies."

"Apologies accepted. And I don't intend to be curt, but I didn't know the man you were during that visit."

"I hardly knew myself, Rebecca. My conduct was rude, condescending, filled with guilt and self-loathing. That is behind me. I realize my error in judgement."

"I am pleased that you do. And forgive me for being so brash, so…so…temperamental. I was not myself, as you were not yourself. Can you forgive me, even though I hold to my decision to not allow you – or anyone else for that matter - to put undeserved guilt on me. Perhaps you should beware that you don't try assigning guilt to anyone else, particularly yourself. You are not guilty; I am not guilty. You are simply injured. But you are still William, the man I love."

"Oh, I forgive you, Rebecca. Additionally, I thank you. I was disturbed at first, even felt that noxious pang of pity for myself, but your words were exactly what I needed. I see clearly now. You were right; you were bold; you were medicinal. You put me on the path of healing, and that healing continues. I thank you. Now, please; may we start over?"

"We can start over regarding that last visit, but I refuse to start over from the beginning. That beginning was too precious, too cherished to require a new beginning. It was fulfilling and exciting. And nothing, save that previous eruption a short while back, has changed. You are still the man I love and want to be a part of my life. I can only hope you feel the same about me."

"The same, Rebecca. I love you and always will. You are a treasure, and I never want to lose you."

"You won't." Rebecca moved closer and kissed William.

Chapter 18

The Settlement

Anna and Sun had left the Keats cabin the day before and were now at Marybeth Wallace's house, the settlement spreading out before them. "This place is growing," Anna had said as they approached the village, log huts sprouting from rocky soil, a blacksmith shop and trading post centering the gathering of other buildings. "It will be a big city someday." Small talk. Something to pass time. Little content. Just chatter. Sun was still wrestling with his demon of revenge and seldom spoke; when he did it was tempered by anger. "They will pay," he had said several times along the way.

Marybeth understood. She listened to the story and agonized with them. "Poor dears," she had said. She shed tears with Anna. The subject of Marybeth and Isaac's upcoming marriage seemed inconsequential at the moment.

"We will go on out to the cabin and see Isaac tomorrow." Anna was able to divert the conversation to something more pleasant after the tears subsided.

"Yes. Isaac will be eager to see you two. He has been completely beside himself at the prospects of your arrival." Marybeth was also beside herself. She was ready to marry Isaac Walker. And while Anna wanted to share with Marybeth the burden of Anna not having a child, she refrained. That could come later, more in the setting of mother and daughter than it was now.

*****

"Good morning, Patience." Isaac was under the big hickory again. Snowball perked her ears in the direction of a rabbit but thought better of it. Seemed Isaac needed her more than she needed a chase. "A beautiful day. God is good. Anna and Jackson should be here soon. Surely wish you could have met Jackson; we call him Sun. A fine young man. Anna loves him with all her being, and he loves her. They haven't faced heartbreak yet, but when they do they have each other and they have God. The three of them will get through life's struggles. In Ecclesiastes Solomon said that thing about a cord of three strands not being easy to break. You remember that, I know."

But they had; they were even now, Anna and Sun, facing heartbreak. They were bruised, disillusioned, wandering and wondering, questioning where God was and who they were. One the other. Wondering: who is this one, this one beside me, on the wagon seat, in my bed, waiting for sleep or passion – or daylight? Why is it so dark? Wandering: trying to find home or solitude or something other than what this journey had brought them.

"Patience, Marybeth and I are getting married. I know that you know, but I just wanted to tell you, to be sure. It now seems right; I look forward to life with her. You remember her – from church. Her husband died before you. You always thought highly of them both. I thank you for giving your permission, but most of all I thank you for showing me what love is." Then Isaac stopped talking and resorted to remembering, to his thoughts, his longings, his own brokenness.

He thought, remembered: *those days that led them here. That long journey that appeared to have no end. That laughter and togetherness. That hardship. Once again, he would like to hold Patience in his arms. To see her smile. To smell her freshly-washed hair and muslin dress. And oh how much he wanted to once again spin his daughter around the campfire as they so often did on the trail between Philadelphia and the frontier cabin.* "Spin me again, Isaac; spin me again." *She had always called him by his name, Isaac, Anna did.*

But Anna was now a woman, not a little girl. No longer could Isaac spin her around the campfire. She would soon be spinning her own children, or watching their father spinning them, around the campfire or Boston or somewhere with which Isaac was not acquainted. That's what Isaac thought. Still, he remembered, thought, wished.

"I love you, Patience. And I love Marybeth. Thank you." Snowball whined.

*****

Daylight found Anna and Sun preparing horses and wagon for a day's travel to the Walker cabin. It would be – they hoped - healing, refreshing, a place of repose from the drain of emotions that had followed them for weeks. Isaac, Snowball, the creek, the mountains, that little pole barn where the rattlesnake had bitten Isaac. Anna came to the rescue, saved Isaac's life. She remembered with clarity her fear, her prayers, her resolve.

She recalled that little half-face from which she had collected a doe that provided meat they needed badly. That had been a long, tortuous journey and a lonely night. But she had accomplished what she set out to do.

She remembered her decorating the cabin for Christmas, that

Christmas not long gone when Sun harmonized on Silent Night. How marvelously well he sings, she recalled thinking. She remembered his coming with her to collect holly boughs and greenery with which to decorate the cabin, how she dismissed him and turned away his efforts of affection.

And she remembered those first weeks in that cabin as newlyweds - the passion, the abandon, the exhilaration of love and bonding and togetherness. She remembered. She longed. And now, right beside her was the one with whom she had shared that togetherness. That one to whom she pledged her love forever; that one who did the same to her. But now, the togetherness felt more like separation. A separation of purpose, of intent, of content even. They will pay hardly seemed an appropriate goal for togetherness.

*****

There, just past a structure and just past the livery station. A figure; a phantom it seemed. Anna felt the chill of horror occupy her entire body. Her breath escaped without warning. No; no. "Sun." That's all Anna could say. Sun. The man she had depended upon, loved, cherished. Now the man she hardly knew.

"Anna?" Sun followed her stare. "That is one of them." Instantly, Sun was charging in the direction of one he considered the most hideous being walking the frontier. "You will pay; you will pay." Sun shouted as he gained distance.

A thunderous blow connected with the man's chin and he crumpled, a tiny cloud of dust rising from the fall. Immediately, Sun sat astraddle the man and pounded angry fists into his face and chest. And before he even realized what he was doing, Sun jerked the big knife from his sash and laid it to the man's throat. "Do you remember me?" Sun shouted, hatred riding his words. "Do you remember me?"

There was no response. Pressure from the knife blade brought a trickle of blood from the man's whiskered neck.

And then soft words, coming from somewhere Sun could not course, from some source outside this circle of hate and violence and evil. Soft words that began slowly to wriggle their way into Sun's disturbed consciousness.

"Sun, I love you. Sun. Sun, I love you. God loves you. God loves even this man beneath you. Sun." Anna didn't plead or shout. She simply talked, softly and affectionately and lovingly and correctly. "Sun."

Sun sat still, the knife's pressure relaxed from the man's throat. Thoughts whirled through Sun's mind. *"How can I do this? How can I not do this?"* He hung his head, then presently sat tall and looked into the man's eyes.

Then recall, more thoughts: *"Careful with that revenge,"* Simon *had said.* *"Not the one you want to give control of your life to."* *Or something similar. It really didn't matter. Sun understood the core of what Simon had said, and Simon was wise. But, still…. The man's breath, foul and shallow on Sun's face. His own rage, red and flaming. His manhood, at least as he saw it, drifting there in the early-autumn air of a place he had never seen. Or had he? This one chance to redeem that manhood, to prove who and what he was.* And then Sun was back, aware.

"Where are your comrades?"

"Scattered I reckon." The man's voice was weak with fear.

"Jesus faced a similar situation." Sun stood, sheathed the knife, brushed frontier dust from his clothes, took Anna's hand and walked away.

*****

And often, after the incident way back along that trail between now and Boston, far away, years ago, maybe it was not that long, back when that Anna was becoming this Anna, she spent restless nights. She would gently crawl from beside Sun, listen briefly to his rhythmic breathing, and secret away. Not far; just away. *They will pay,* Sun's words, were a constant in her tortured mind. *They must pay,* her thought, was even more disruptive.

Must they pay – here, in this world, on this frontier? Is God listening? How did I lose Him? But He did rescue me, didn't He? From those men. And He rescued me from myself, when I was a child. Saved me, gave me life, even eternal life. And Isaac and Sun and Simon and… everyone who turns to Him in repentance, in belief, in acceptance of His Son. He did; He will. Perhaps it was I who moved, who wandered into doubt and anger. Yes, it must be.

But why no child? I miss Isaac; I miss home; I miss Snowball. I miss who I was. Same process on each night-time journey into despair and hoped-for hope. Anna kept searching for God, for Sun; she had known both well. She would then return to Sun, before he awoke and found her missing, before he roused to head into another day of clouds with no rain, into another day of shallows in search of depth.

*****

Richard Montgomery's expedition, one of two moving with the intent to invade Quebec, left Fort Ticonderoga late August, 1775. This proposed invasion would be the first major effort by the new Continental Army. Benedict Arnold led a separate expedition that left Cambridge in early September. The two, Arnold's and Montgomery's, would later meet at Quebec City. Reports revealed that Arnold's expedition encountered tremendous hardship negotiating wilderness conditions in Maine, and forces were much reduced.

In mid-September, Montgomery's troops began the siege of Fort St. Johns, a strategic stronghold. The Fort was not taken until November. It was there that British General Carleton barely avoided capture and fled to Quebec City. Both the Montgomery and Arnold forces suffered defeat in December 1775 at the Battle of Quebec.

Chapter 19

Road to Walker cabin Mid September

"Battles must surely be raging by now." Sun spoke softly, his mind muddled, tormented. September's promise of a glorious autumn yet to impact his anguish.

"But not just in the war." Anna whispered, as if allowing a thought to morph into voiced form without permission.

I'm sorry; I was distracted. What did you say?"

"Battles," Anna sighed.

"What about battles, Anna?"

"You said battles were raging."

"Yes. The war, I am sure, is growing in intensity. And in ferocity I fear."

"It likely is."

"But you said not just in war, Anna. What did you mean? I don't understand."

"Those other battles, not war battles but just as harmful." Anna turned and stared at a sweetgum leaf that was already changing into something more suitable for an autumn celebration. A yellow gown with tiny brown borders. She kept her gaze there and spoke in a somber tone, melancholy wrapping each word in shadows of despondency. "Battles that rend the spirit with the same efficacy musket balls rend the body." She fell silent, studying that leaf and wondering where peace had gone, whether smiles and warmth would ever return, if she – they – would once again find God.

"Battles that rend the spirit?" Jackson seemed puzzled. I'm not sure…. I…."

"As surely as musket balls." Anna had lost sight of that one particular leaf as the wagon moved forward, but she continued her distant gazing. Perhaps there was something out there, somewhere out there, that would help her mend. *"Hope deferred maketh the heart sick; but when the desire cometh, it is a tree of life."* Anna remembered Proverbs 13:12. Her heart was sick; Sun's heart was sick. They needed that tree of life.

"Battles of life apart from war; is that what you mean?"

"That is what I mean. It seems we two are in the middle of battle with no redoubt to protect us." Anna was honest, troubled.

"Yes." Sun breathed the word out as if he were fatigued, minus energy to do more than stare. "How is it that a reasonably few days can affect such perplexing turmoil? Can transport one from happiness to agitation? Can replace secure contentment with foreboding unease? How?"

"At this moment, I have no viable answers. Life, I suppose. Life does not promise perfection."

*****

Walker Cabin

Dusk was too quickly approaching. Isaac Walker stood on the porch of his cabin, Snowball sitting at his side. An owl hooted – forlorn, distant but close, or so it seemed. A tardy squirrel chattered, scurried up rough bark and buried itself in a leaf nest. Isaac, and Snowball, looked toward the settlement, then toward the creek, then toward the mountains over there, then toward that big, lonesome hickory. They should be here by now. Not spoken. Just a thought, a hope, an ache.

*****

"We must put on our best faces." Anna finally spoke. The most recent miles and hours had passed in silence, save the squeak of harness and chattering of birds, and thoughts – if they could be heard.

"Best faces?" Sun seemed to have again drifted into some cavernous abyss of detachment. Anna's abyss could well be named *Abandonment*.

"Yes, best faces. For Marybeth and Isaac."

"Yes, of course. For them." Sun was present and absent and caring and aloof, all simultaneously.

"It is their wedding. We have no right to dampen that, to express our lostness." Anna said it, but already she was not certain that she was completely lost, not like before, not like those first days after that sobering intrusion. When was it? She couldn't recall. Perhaps the frontier and Snowball and Marybeth and Isaac would be the answers she needed, the course to wholeness that would remove her lostness. Would restore her confidence, her faith. But her faith was still there, shaded in dark shadows but there.

"Yes. Suggestions, my dear?" That detachment again.

"Our best faces. We must put on our best faces."

"Yes. Our best faces." Walker Cabin came into view.

*****

Keats Cabin

"Shorely am worried 'bout them youngsters, Nora Jean." Simon was sincere, gentle.

"So am I, Simon" Nora Jean didn't chastise Simon for his long-hunter speech, didn't trouble him about meddling. This time, there was no doubt, he was not meddling. He was heartbroken.

"That thing back there, on the trail toward Boston, it was more'n hurtful; it was plumb nigh unbearable, nerve shatterin' and flat-out gruesome. How them young folks gonna pull outta' this?"

"They have faith, Simon. And they know God." Nora Jean was reassuring.

"They shorely do; shorely do. But I done been in them dark places, Nora Jean. 'Spect you have too. I done been whur faith's plumb wore out and God can't be found nowhur, ain't makin' a sound. That's the way it seems anyhow. He can't be found and's quiet as a mouse creeping 'round the cupboard. 'Course you and me know He ain't gone nowhur. He's right there whur we done left Him but shorely don't feel that way sometimes. Shorely don't."

"Indeed, Simon. I know. Prayer and rest and contemplation and searching will lead them back. They must be allowed to wonder and sort things out minus condemnation. Time and God, Simon. That's what they need."

"You shorely are smartsome, Nora Jean. Even ole Simon Keats couldn't a' said it just rightly better'n you did. Shorely couldn't."

*****

Walker Cabin

Anna and Isaac fell immediately into a locked embrace; the

wagon had hardly stopped. That embrace was expected, welcomed but directly became alarming, alarming for Isaac anyway. Isaac was crying, tears of joy they were. But Anna was weeping - shaking and heaving and torn with excruciation. No words other than *Isaac*. Whispered, slipping quietly from a constricted throat. Sun remained stoic. With each lap, her back legs seeming to rush ahead of her front, Snowball decreased the circumference of boisterous circles and eventually closed to lick any hand that might dangle in her direction. No takers. She resigned to whining.

"Anna. Dear Anna." Isaac needed not say more. Anna thought those the most precious words she had ever heard.

Their story, told to Isaac later that evening around the candle-lit table, an occasional flicker of a small fire at the hearth, was one of anguish, lost direction, lack of purpose. And while the subject was not broached, there was misplaced passion – Anna for Sun, Sun for Anna, for life itself, both them. Passion misplaced. Passion that had fallen victim to anger, revenge, confusion – fear even. Isaac was, as they, somber, crushed. Words failed him.

"Oh my. Dear, dear Anna and Sun," was all he could manage. The night wore on.

"I will excuse myself to the half-face and leave you two the cabin. The weather is pleasant, and Snowball will join me." Isaac had finally found a scattering of words. "And with your permission, I'll go to the settlement tomorrow. I need to see Marybeth."

"Of course, Isaac." Jackson Bain had become a man of limited conversation lately.

But Snowball did not join Isaac. She curled on the porch, hard against the cabin door. Chin on forepaws. Sad eyes. Distraught.

Chapter 20

The Settlement

"I heard, Isaac." Marybeth met him at the door, pleased to see him and yet troubled. "Anna and Jackson. How could someone do that to them? What should we do for them?"

"I share your concern, Marybeth." Isaac spoke with compassion.

"Oh, Isaac. You are a caring and gentle man. I love you."

"And I love you as well; very much. You asked what we should do. We should pray for them, love them, support them, and primarily allow them to work through this without our judging or prodding. That is what we should do."

"Yes. That is what we should do." Marybeth smiled.

"And we, as they, should get along with this business of living. That is a profitable route through the forest of despair. And we should plan a wedding; we should get married. You do still want to marry me, don't you, Marybeth?" Isaac's voice and face carried a hint of joviality.

"More than anything else, I want to marry you. Today would be perfect." Marybeth leaned close and kissed Isaac.

"What about in a week or more? Say the last Saturday in September, Marybeth. Will that suit you?"

"That's too far off, but I've been waiting...." Marybeth paused and pointed a teasing finger in Isaac's face. "What are you doing standing around here like a lovesick youngster? Get out and go speak to Reverend Sullivan. We have a wedding to schedule. Now, off with you, Isaac Walker!"

*****

Boston

"You are...alluring, captivating, incredibly beautiful. And you own my heart, Rebecca." William Clarkson wasted no time when Rebecca Bomar opened the door.

"Well, now, William. Feel free to tell me how you really feel." Rebecca teased, twirled a lock of hair, smiled demurely. "Please, come in. We'll go to the parlor." She led the way. "Let's sit on the sofa." Rebecca sat.

"Before I sit there beside you, please assist me. I haven't attempted this maneuver since that miserable musket ball introduced itself, so I am not certain I can manage it properly without help. Either way, it won't be terribly graceful. William began an unsure task that he hoped would eventually put him in a knelling position. Rebecca stood and held his arm. "Now, that's it. Thank you. Please, have a seat."

Rebecca did as he asked and sat open mouthed, her mind spinning with confusion – and glee, though she feared that latter was ill placed. "What on earth are you doing, William?"

"We have talked of our love and have even mentioned marriage, but I recently realized I had left out a strategic portion of the entire process. I shall rectify that immediately." William exuded pleasantness, joy.

"William, are you...?"

"You must wait and see if I am."

"By all means, William. Please continue."

"I love you. I want to spend the remainder of my life with you. So I ask, with absolutely no doubts, no hesitation, and with great anticipation, will you marry me, Rebecca Bomar?"

"William Clarkson, it would be my pleasure to marry you. Yes; yes; yes!" Rebecca leaned forward and kissed William – with all her heart.

*****

Walker Cabin

"I hurt for Isaac, Sun. I mean, he was exceedingly hopeful for our return and fully excited about his upcoming marriage to Marybeth and we came to him broken, tormented, bringing our burden, seeking solace in this, his, beautiful world. I hurt for him." Anna fell silent.

"Yes." Sun volunteered nothing more.

"I love Isaac more than I can say. He has and would again do anything within his power for me - and for you too, Sun. Anything. I am grieved for him."

"Yes." One word from Sun, the same as before. Anna pled - inside, not with words - for more. Her thought: *Where is he, this man I pledged my heart, my life to? Sun? Where is he?*

"Sun, are we lost? Is our faith dead? Has life so wounded us that we are simply no more, gone, destined to wander a scorched desert of emptiness? Sun?" A long silence. Only the sound of an autumn breeze. Snowball barking from the porch at a deer down by the creek.

The rattling chirp of grasshoppers.

"Isaac will be in the settlement two days." Anna was not sure why she even mentioned this. Just something to say, she guessed. But Sun didn't say – not a word, not even a grunt of recognition. He simply didn't say. He did wander onto the porch and patted Snowball's head.

*****

Restlessness got the better of Anna that night – the night following Isaac's leaving for the settlement, the night following her foiled efforts to engage Sun in conversation, the night that, she now concluded, would never give way to daylight. She eased from the bed, beside Sun but not with nor of Sun. He put his hand on her shoulder. "Just need to go outside – alone," she whispered. Sun rolled over.

Now off the porch and down the trail toward the creek. And soaring high above it all as a spectator, looking down on the grandeur of God's handiwork and her home and Snowball – and misery. The beauty and the ugliness. That's what she imagined herself doing anyway, wished she could do. Snowball came, a wet and gentle nose pressed to Anna's hand, leaning, with slow-wagging tail and questioning eyes, against Anna's knee.

"Sorry, Girl. I haven't been kind to you. Unconditional love; that's what you have. Oh, but how we humans need to take a lesson from you." Anna rubbed Snowball's head and ears, even knelt and pulled Snowball into an embrace. "We need a lesson, Girl." Anna prayed.

"Lord, I have let my faith falter; I have doubted you; I have let disappointment and anger and hardship and fear control my life. God, forgive me. Heal me; heal Sun. Mend our hearts and lead us on the correct path. I know you are there, God. It is I who has wandered.

I recognize and praise your greatness. Touch me, Lord; touch Sun. I know you are there."

The night sky was brilliant. Stars formed a textured canopy that invited one to settle into quiet sleep among them – if one could actually do that. The moon reclined, or so it seemed, on mountains in the distance. Autumn's sweet breath rustled through changing leaves and brought that refreshing that only autumn can bring. Anna turned toward the cabin.

"I watched you." Sun was waiting on the porch. "I watched you go down by the creek and rub Snowball and stand there looking up-ward. The moon provided ample light, so I just watched. What were you doing?" Sun was agreeably gentle, no anger riding his manner.

"Praying." Anna, much as Sun had been earlier, had little to say. Still, she was encouraged by his willingness to say something – any-thing, anything but silence.

"I suppose I was doing likewise. Not down on my knees and pleading with God but at least again remembering that He existed, was present, even though I have doubted that recently. So, I was pray-ing, in an odd sort of way I guess. Watching you, watching Snowball, watching the night sky. Looking for God."

"Did you find Him?"

"Not entirely, but I did see quiet glimpses in all that I saw – you, Snowball, the night sky. He was there. I'm yet a long way removed and struggling to find my way, but He is there. Waiting."

"That is good to hear. And me too, the same as you said." Anna walked up the steps and held Sun.

"Anna, I need you."

"And I need you, Sun."

"What happened? What is still happening? Are we fully lost?" Sun was raising bold and possibly painful questions, but questions that screamed for attention.

"I don't know that I have answers, certainly not one single answer that would satisfy those questions. I do know that we, at least I, drifted away. Partly because of that horrid incident, but also because of inner struggles. But I do know that we are not fully lost. Turned around on the trail and a bit confused, but not fully lost. With God's help, we will find our way. I need your help, Sun."

"And I need your help, Anna. Please, let's go inside and lie down. There are two hours remaining before sunrise. Join me. I need you."

"I will glady join you." Anna felt warmth.

They, Anna and Sun, presently found themselves melded, one, sharing, partners, lovers. Life had not ended.

*****

"The last Saturday of September." Isaac couldn't restrain himself. He hardly proffered a greeting before those words took wing and flew from his mouth. "Reverend Sullivan is spreading the word. At the church in the settlement - that's where we'll have the ceremony. And the reception will be on the grounds outside. It will be a genuine frontier gala. And Marybeth is…."

"Slow down, Isaac." Anna teased as she spoke. "We can get the details as needed. First, I must ask you a question."

"Yes, Yes. Go right ahead. Ask whatever you wish. The main thing is that Marybeth and I are getting married. We will live in the settlement, at least for a while, and we will laugh and love and celebrate and…."

"Easy, Isaac. Breathe; breathe. Slowly; deeply. Calm down." Sun smiled and jabbed Isaac's shoulder with an outstretched finger. "Anna has a question."

"Yes. Ask away, Girl."

"My question: Isaac, are you excited?" Laughter – from them all. Snowball's tail wag was filled with enthusiasm.

Chapter 21

The Settlement

Although simple, the wedding was an exercise in perfection. No recitations forgotten, no foibles from anyone participating. Perfection. However, Isaac was somewhat abashed when Reverend Sullivan told him he could kiss Marybeth. Still, he completed his pleasant chore with grandiosity. Guests cheered. Simon Keats' voice could be heard above the din when he shouted, "That Isaac Walker shorely is somethin'. He shorely is!"

Marybeth was breathtaking – as brides are. Poised, graceful – she walked down the aisle wearing an immense smile and met Isaac at the front, her eyes like glowing pools. Glinting diamonds, they appeared. Marybeth's demeanor revealed that she not only loved Isaac Walker but was eager to share her life with him.

Lizza McDougall was ecstatic. She squirmed and preened and toyed with spiraling curls, so much so that Reverend Sullivan coughed softly once, this after daring a fleeting glance at her and feeling his heart flutter and his mind drift into the realm of carnal matters. But he grasped at his escaping composure and snatched it back before all was lost. Perhaps no one noticed. Mrs. Franklinton had noticed. She cleared her throat and scowled.

Promptly – Lizza thought it ages – Reverend Sullivan declared Isaac and Marybeth husband and wife. "Join me in prayer," he said. And afterward, "Ladies and gentlemen, I am pleased to introduce Mr. and Mrs. Isaac Walker." The congregation cheered. The newlyweds walked out of the church to soft congratulations and admiring smiles.

"Yessiree." Simon was his usual boisterous self. "That Isaac Walker shorely is…." Nora Jean punched an elbow into Simon's side.

"And I invite you all to join the happy couple for a frontier party like no other. Just out there in front." Reverend Sullivan gestured. "Please join us. Thank you, and you are dismissed."

*****

Wooden tables were gathered in neat clusters. Blankets and baskets scattered about added to the festivity. Children scudded, little boys chasing little girls, the latter releasing high-pitched squeals and thinking their pursuers quite juvenile – though they did not know that word. Young teenagers clustered, boys over here, girls over there. Unspoken words and contemplation of preference and selection and intrigue and desire to mingle stirred among them, but only within their bubbles of familiarity. Male and female were yet mysterious territory.

Marybeth and Isaac stood and received well wishes. Men smiled and winked at Isaac, prodding him with an elbow or shoulder. Women admonished him to care for and love Marybeth. Some of these same wiped tears as they hugged her. All completed their congratulations, subtle as well as gleeful, and gathered on the grounds in small assemblages and around tables filled with culinary delights. The bonfire roared; fiddle and fife began to play – waltzes and Scottish reels and familiar folk tunes.

"Shameful," Mrs. Franklinton approached Reverend Sullivan. "You are my Reverend, but I shall scold you as if you were my grandson. Shameful, I tell you."

"My apologies, Mrs. Franklinton. I regret your feeling that way, but I must plead innocent to your innuendos, or at least ignorant. I am sorry, but I don't fully understand." Liam Sullivan was sincere in his approach and was certainly not taken by surprise. He had encountered Mrs. Franklinton's ire before, as had the bulk of the settlement's population. The woman had her own peculiar list of what she considered improprieties, and according to the shared sentiments of most, she too often chastised. "Perhaps you should thoroughly explain."

"I shall be happy to do so, young man. This is scandalous, this… this…this carrying on with that McDougall lass." Mrs. Franklinton spat the words with pronounced vigor. "You know the one, that one with red hair. You must curtail such action or we shall run you from this settlement forthwith. Scandalous, I tell you. Scandalous." Save a wagging finger poked precariously close to Reverend Sullivan's nose, Mrs. Franklinton fell silent.

Liam thought carefully before speaking. *You and who else will run me from the settlement? You and those other two gossipers within your sorority? What are you saying, woman?* These were only words that flitted through his mind; he would not voice them. *Lord, forgive me. My attitude is not one pleasing to you.* Now he would speak.

"Yes, or course. Lizza McDougall." Liam was gentle. "A fine young lady and an active member of this congregation. Oscar and Matilda's daughter. What about Lizza, Mrs. Franklinton?"

"Yes; that is the one. That L-i-z-z-a." Mrs. Franklinton's eyes spoke disapproval. "I see the way you look at her, and I see her looking back. If you ask me, this is fully inappropriate and should not be tolerated. We shall run…."

"And what do you deduce is inappropriate about this, Mrs. Franklinton?"

"Why, Mr. Franklinton - God rest his soul - and I were married before he even held my hand. And here you and this McDougall lass are flitting about and doing who knows what, and it is completely inappropriate. I can only imagine what you two...."

"Well, perhaps your imagination is running too freely, too wildly, Mrs. Franklinton. Do you have facts that support your assumptions?"

"I need no facts. I just know, and what I know is that this is entirely unacceptable."

"It is true that Lizza McDougall and I are courting, and with her parents' permission I must say, but our actions are not inappropriate, are not an affront to God or members of this community. We want to honor God, to follow His leading. Now if you will kindly excuse me, I shall go about visiting with other wedding guests."

"I will not excuse you, Reverend. I have much more to say and you would do well to listen."

"I'm sorry, Mrs. Franklinton. I really must be going. I shall take your words under advisement. Good evening, Mrs. Franklinton."

"Well, I never." Mrs. Franklinton huffed. "The only way you can redeem yourself is to take that girl to wife. Even then, the scandal will persist. I never...." Mrs. Franklinton turned and paced hastily away from Reverend Liam Sullivan, her nose high and lips pursed.

"I plan to do just that." Liam smiled and waved her goodbye; she didn't hear nor see. "I plan to do that soon."

*****

The night wore well. Bright sky, dancing, feasting, laughing, fellowship. Marybeth and Isaac moved casually among the guests, thanking them and bidding them goodnight. They, the newlyweds, were seen walking toward Marybeth's house, hand in hand. Children began to tire. Simon Keats proffered once more his pronouncement: "That Isaac Walker shorely is somethin'. He's shorely somethin'."

"Ladies and Gentlemen." Reverend Sullivan asked for attention. "This has been a grand night. I invite you to have one last waltz before you go. And I invite Lizza McDougall to join me in that waltz. Immediately following, and before you leave, please allow me to make one last announcement." He gathered Lizza, moved toward the dimming bonfire and requested the fiddle and fife to play. They waltzed beautifully.

While others joined them initially, the two, Lizza and Liam, soon had the full admiration of everyone else; a large circle formed around them. But the couple hardly noticed. They were immersed in other thoughts. Lizza of Liam, Liam of Lizza. The music stopped before the two recognized they were the only dancers remaining. All others were now spectators. Reverend Sullivan composed himself, a wide smile growing with intensity.

"Yes, a grand night. And with your permission, all you my friends and most of you my congregants, I wish, before the festivities end, to make an announcement." Whispers and nods arose throughout. Liam peeked about in an effort to locate Mrs. Franklinton.

"As you know, Lizza McDougal and I, with the permission of Matilda and Oscar, have been courting. But what you probably do not know is that I have asked her to be my wife." A shout form somewhere in the crowd. "And I am delighted to note that she accepted." More shouts, one clearly from Simon Keats. "So with her permission, I now invite you to a wedding the first week of December. The specific date will be forthcoming. Again to all, thank you for sharing this celebration, and good night." Mrs. Franklinton was not to be seen.

Lizza stood close to Liam. The crowd began to head home, some of them carrying little ones, these little ones sleeping peacefully. The bonfire was now a mere whimper of what it had been, but its coals glowed brightly. An abstract portrait of the hearts of Lizza and Liam.

Chapter 22

Settlement Church

Sunday morning broke clear. Autumn was exerting dominance across the frontier, leaves dressing for a grand ballet that would begin any time now. It was, all must have concluded, based on the numbers who were trickling into the church, a glorious day, one encouraging worship.

"I did not expect to see you two this morning," one man whispered to Isaac Walker outside the church. Marybeth showed a hint of chagrin. She smiled.

"Oh, we would not have missed this for anything." Isaac was resolute.

"No. We would not have missed it." Marybeth looked with affection into Isaac's eyes. "It is a superb day."

Inside, church folk were taking their seats, silence already reigning over the audible comradery of moments earlier. Reverend Sullivan took the podium and began.

"Welcome everyone; welcome, indeed. This is an extraordinary day the Lord has made. I invite you to celebrate His goodness and blessing. And in the unlikely event that some of you are not aware, we welcome a new couple into our midst. Oh, they have been with us for some time now, but they were then here individually. They are here today in their first service as husband and wife. Isaac, Marybeth - so very good to see you." There were smiles and head nods throughout. "And after a prayer to inaugurate this service, I invite you to turn in your Bibles to the Psalms, number 121 it is." Liam prayed.

"Stand with me for the reading." Reverend Liam Sullivan's resonant voice belied his still-young age. "'*I will lift up mine eyes unto the hills, from whence cometh my help.*'" Reverend Sullivan paused. "Now look carefully at this next verse, verse two." '*My help cometh from the LORD, which made heaven and earth.*' The psalmist gets to the heart of the matter quickly. His help, our help, comes from nothing or no one other than the LORD. That will be the focus of this message."

The Reverend discussed that God never slumbered, that He was the keeper and protector, that He preserved. God is and will be the abiding source of help, for now and for evermore. The congregation was attentive, followed his reading and his every word. He closed the service with a blessing and stood outside to speak with those present.

"Good message," some said.

"You are welcome to join us for a meal, Reverend," others opined.

"Thank you for reminding us that God is our only true help and security," one man offered.

And then they were gone – on foot, on horseback, in wagons loaded with squirming children and aging adults. Anna and Sun headed to the Walker cabin, quietly at first, but Liam's sermon would coax them to conversation.

*****

"He is right, you know." Anna was contemplative.

116

"I'm sorry, Anna. I was daydreaming. No, I was thinking about Liam's sermon. What did you say?" Sun had become much more engaging in recent days than he had been along the trail and after that incident.

"Reverend Sullivan. He is right. God is our help. Even in the midst of His grand creation - the hills, the rivers, the wild things – it is God who is our only true help. We can enjoy and appreciate all He made and be refreshed by it, like here on the frontier that is so entirely pleasant, but it is ultimately God Himself who is our hope, our help, our salvation. We simply must never forget or neglect Him. He is now and forever, and we are lost sheep without His strong hands of guidance and uplifting."

"Well said, Anna. I concur. We must never lose sight of that. Never…again." Sun looked away as if ashamed.

"Again, Sun?"

"Yes. Again. I fear we have, at least I have, recently…."

"Not only you, Sun. I have as well – forgotten God's goodness and protection and love. And if not forgotten, then surely neglected. Because of anger or disillusionment or fear or whatever brought it. I have failed. My primary failure is that I have forgotten or neglected my recognition of who God really is. He is the one true God, worthy of my praise and worship. Worthy of my dedication and service. Regardless of what happens. I am sorry, Sun. And God," Anna turned her face toward the heavens, "I am sorry. Forgive me."

"And me as well, God. And Anna, you too. Forgive me."

"I forgive you, Sun. And God forgives all who repent of their sins and turn to Him. We both, you and I, are forgiven." Anna sat close to Sun; the wagon rattled toward Walker cabin – home.

*****

McDougall Cabin

"I have checked schedules and plans and talked with friends and I think the first Friday evening of December would be perfect. That won't interfere with Christmas celebrations. What do you think, Liam?" Lizza was effervescent, energetic. Her red hair hung in ringlets, accentuating a vibrant face made more so by smiling lips and inviting eyes.

"That meets my favor completely. I shall arrange for a guest speaker to conduct services that Sunday following our wedding." Liam was as excited and expectant as was Lizza – if that were remotely possible. Lizza seemed perpetually excited and expectant.

"That would be wise, my dear. You shall be in no condition to conduct service that soon after the ceremony. And remember, I will begin lessons on preaching only minutes after the wedding. You should wait for that tutorial - and many more to follow – before you again take the pulpit. You will be forever changed, your preaching certain to improve from its now stellar form." Lizza giggled.

"Oh my, Lizza. What am I to do with you?"

"Fewer than three months and I shall show you what you are to do! Patience, dear one. Patience." Lizza twirled and teased as Liam watched, mouth open and eyes sparkling.

*****

Walker Cabin – Two Weeks Later

That bond of passion and warmth between Anna and Sun had enjoyed revival. They talked and shared and embraced enthusiastically. This morning they sat on the porch of the cabin, and there, in the distance, hills were filling with autumn's splendor. The creek wore a thin blanket of sleepy, off-cast foliage, this drifting in taciturn reflection with a gentle current. Vibrant color displayed in every direction. Anna lifted a sweetgum leaf from near her moccasin toe - lovingly, tenderly.

"Beautiful." Her one-word affirmation exhibited a depth of character.

"Yes you are." Sun smiled.

"I meant the leaf; it is beautiful."

"I concur it is, but I meant you. Beautiful. More beautiful than ever. And you shall continue to grow in your beauty as time passes."

"Oh, Sun; you are too kind to me. But I thank you. I love you. And it is so very pleasant to have you back."

"And so very pleasant to be back. And to have you back I must say. Very pleasant."

"Yes, we both drifted away for a while. It was a frightening and empty place, not the place I wanted to be. We must always guard against that drifting, must maintain that hold on ourselves and most importantly allow God to maintain His hold on us. Never again should we drift as we did." Anna took Sun's hand.

"Never again, Anna. I agree. Never again." Sun leaned in and kissed Anna. A flock of geese overhead performed a visual symphony as they progressed southward. "Walk with me," Sun said presently. He stood, took Anna's hand and escorted her from the porch.

"Where are we going?"

"Oh, I can't say for certain. But I can say for certain that wherever I go I want you with me." Sun put his arm around Anna's shoulders.

"Same with me." They walked – close and loving and caring, a strong bond growing even stronger.

"Anna," Sun was deliberate. "You are aware of the situation with my father, but I am not convinced you are aware of its gravity. I fear I have held some things back from you. For that I am sorry. But I now

want to lay all the details out before you, to have you fully in touch
with what transpired. This latest breach of faith – and communication
I must add – that we experienced as a result of that ghastly incident
along the trail has taught me to trust more and to be open to you and
to God. I want to tell it all. I hope this will not be too terribly painful."

"Pain is a common ingredient of living, Sun. I shall listen with
empathy and minus judgement. Please, carry on."

"You recognized, I am sure, that tension when my mother
broached the issue of my father during her introduction and welcome
back at Bain House before we left on this most recent journey. She
came precariously close to dealing with a matter that has been conjecture since that excruciating loss of little Alice. She died in that wagon
fire you will recall."

"Yes; yes. Purely unthinkable. Horrible."

"That it was. And complete healing will likely never come for
this family, particularly for Cora and Robert. But what exacerbates
the loss is that my father was almost surely the instigator of that sor-
did affair." Sun paused and looked at Anna.

"I feared that to be the case. There has been little confirmation
as I understand, but I deduced that might be the suspicion." Anna's
demeanor exhibited remorse.

"Yes, definitely. My father was a powerful man who grew accustomed to having things go his way, and he intended for nothing or
no one to impede his conclusions and decisions. Robert had left the
employ of Bain Enterprises to launch a freight business – with Cora's
full support, of course. But my father failed to share the same enthusiasm. For whatever reasons, he was adamantly opposed to such an
endeavor."

"I decided that to be the case early on."

"It was. Evidence, or perhaps it was little more than conjecture,
indicated that my father hired some unsavory individual to fire the

wagons and that first load to dissuade any promise of success for Jamison Freight, in hopes that Cora and Robert would return and remain under his suffocating hold. Not that he felt his control was suffocating. He just saw it as protection and security for Cora and her children. But his was a suffocating hold nonetheless."

"Oh, Sun. How disconcerting. I am truly sorry."

"Now, never would I suggest that he even considered any harm might come to them save that loss of equipment and goods. He was in no way vile in regards to that degree of loss and suffering. He was just blinded by his own controlling nature. Anna, that was a perfect example of allowing emotions and preconceived notions to get the better of understanding and logic, love and respect as well, and it ultimately led to destruction. In fact, I surmise that the news of Alice's tragedy was directly responsible for Father's sudden decline and ultimate death."

"I can't…. I…." Anna was without comment.

"And another matter that I am embarrassed to even mention in light of the greater loss of little Alice and the dreams of Cora and Robert is that my father attempted to cajole and control me as well. When he learned that I was not going to move immediately into the business with him after returning from my university studies in the Mother Country, he spoke tortuous words capable of demolishing the spirit: 'I have no son,' he said. Oh, Anna, it was…."

"An adequate response escapes me, Sun. How horribly hurtful. I simply cannot imagine the impact of such a statement. Just know that I cherish and love you."

"I know that – fully. And I cherish and love you. But Anna, I have not dealt with this as I should have, as I must. Father and I reconciled a few days before he died, or I attempted reconciliation at least, and I am convinced that he recognized God's love and accepted Jesus as his Savior. But I didn't then nor have I yet forgiven him. I mean fully forgiven him. I must do that. So Anna, I am asking you to right now pray with me and for days to come pray for me. I must release this and give it to God if I am to move forward in full favor and in full contact with God and with you. Will you do that – pray with me now and for me tomorrow and the next day and the next? Will you?"

"Gladly, Sun. Gladly. Those days and all days to come. I will." They stopped there by the creek and dropped to their knees.

Chapter 23

Late October

There could be no doubt that autumn was surrendering to the belligerent coaxing of winter. The color show was at its peak, but there was that familiar something in the air that indicated this most pleasant and inviting of all seasons would slide away behind the hills like an evening sunset and with little more than a faint whimper any day now. Still, autumn was in control – for a short while longer anyway. The frontier folk were celebrating but making ready for cold, for snow, for more hours beside the hearth.

"Time to make meat." Sun was jovial and pulled Anna close - his smile warming her, Anna's touch warming him. I'll check with Oscar McDougall and Webster Jacobson. Perhaps they would like to make this a neighborly effort."

"That they will, Sun. And I'm sure we women and the children will enjoy some quiet time minus the useless chatter and boisterous clatter of menfolk gathering for the hunt" Anna pretended disgust.

"True, but the Jacobson and McDougall boys should be ready by now to follow along with the men. They have to learn, and this is a good time to start."

"Yes, of course. And that will make our woman time even more pleasant."

"I'm sure. But if I recall, you are quite the hunter yourself, Anna. Perhaps you could join us as well."

"I think not. And my hunting was at a time when I had to take dramatic measures to save Isaac and me, but I much prefer to be more domestic." Anna smiled. "And besides, there is a tiny flutter in my belly today, and I opt to be with the women when the hunt takes place.

"A flutter?"

"Yes. It is most certainly those butterflies that I feel each time you smile and hold me." Anna touched Sun's cheek with affection.

"Oh, so very good to have you say that about this confused and often-lost husband you endure daily. So very good." Sun pulled Anna close and looked into her eyes.

"And Anna, I gave Liam a letter in hopes he could get it to the right person or persons so that it would be delivered to Boston. I advised the family that you and I would not be back there immediately. I can only hope that letter finds its way safely to them."

"So do I. That is never a certainty from the settlement. And since you mention it, when do you think we will try to go back? I know you would like to be there for Christmas, but that is not now possible." Anna showed her genuine concern for the entire Bain family – and particularly for Sun.

"No, that won't be possible. I would think we need to wait until spring. I can only guess how the conflict is progressing back there, and winter travel is difficult. Additionally, I don't see the two of us up to such a journey right now. We need rest, reflection, quiet surroundings. I hope that is not selfish, and I am burdened for my family."

"Not selfish at all, Sun. We would be ill prepared to try that now. Yes, we need rest. We need time to heal and perhaps do some rediscovering."

"Rediscovering, Anna?"

"Yes. Rediscovering God and ourselves. Our own relationship. Our relationship with God. All is much better now, but we are yet wounded." Anna was correct. Those yawning relationship gaps between the two of them and between them, individually and as a couple, and God still held them in an icy grip, still gnawed and scowled and threatened. They needed time.

"Agreed, Anna. And time we shall have – here in this grand frontier, this land of healing. You and I have healed here before, and we shall heal here again."

*****

Early November

Since their wedding, Marybeth and Isaac had twice visited Anna and Sun. They limited their stays to one night each trip, for the Walker Cabin was less than ideal for two couples. Still, they talked and laughed and remembered around a robust oak fire on those blustery, early-winter evenings.

"So, you are coming here again next week to join this raucous frontier gathering for the hunt, Papa?" Anna did not restrain that tone of plea in her voice.

"Yes, of course. I wouldn't miss that for anything. But there is one condition." Isaac looked at Anna and then at Sun and then at Marybeth. "We want you, Anna and Sun, to be our guests at Thanksgiving. And plan to stay over for church that Sunday following. We have ample room back there in the settlement. Can you two do that?"

"Yes, Papa; we can do that. Can't we, Sun?"

"We can, and gladly. Thank you for the invitation. It will be a glorious time of giving thanks."

"That it will." Marybeth entered the conversation. "And Anna, we will have the food. You need do nothing other than be our guest."

"Thank you. And Marybeth, will you come with Isaac when he comes for the hunt? We women will gather at the Jacobsons and talk about how these men so poorly treat us. You wouldn't want to miss that, would you?" They all laughed.

"I wouldn't want to miss that; no. But I must say that I have never been a part of 'making meat' as some folks call it, but I would enjoy the companionship of the ladies. Yes, I will come."

"But Marybeth, be advised that we women do participate in some of the work. We make the jerked meat and we salt bear bacon and keep hungry hunters fed. So, this is not simply a group of intelligent females discussing deep matters of philosophy and theology – though we do all that with abandon and thorough comprehension. We work alongside the men at several points throughout the process." Anna patted Marybeth's shoulder.

"Yes, yes; I understand. But since I am definitely not skilled in making meat, I restrict myself to the job of gripper." Marybeth raised her eyebrows.

"Gripper? What is that?" Sun was blindsided by Marybeth's comment.

"Well, if someone says, 'Here, you hold this,' I shall happily comply. I can grip whatever is given me."

"All right; you got me on that one." Sun put his face in his hands and pretended embarrassment.

"Say, Isaac; have you heard from Simon? Will he join us on this adventure?" Sun was hopeful.

"I have seen him once since the wedding. He came into the settlement and before he left it was anything but settled, if you know what I mean."

"We know," Anna added.

"Conditions went from tranquil to near unnerving upon his arrival. He came in shouting and slapping his leg and laughing so loudly that I heard deer snorting and elk bugling two mountains away. Goodness; that man can be obnoxious, but he is the dearest soul I've ever known. This world would be far less palatable without Simon Keats in it. Wise, loving, compassionate – I don't have ample words to describe how I feel about him."

"Agreed, Isaac." Sun felt the same about Simon as did Isaac. "I owe him a tremendous debt of gratitude. And did he mention the hunt?"

"He did. To quote him, 'Shorely is 'bout time for you youngsters to make meat. Shorely is. And iffin I could I'd join you all 'cause I got the smartsomes to show ever'body how to hunt right, what with bein' so skilledful and all like I am.' You know Simon. He is never short of praise for himself." Isaac paused.

"We know him quite well." Anna this time.

"But," Isaac continued, "he said he would not likely join us. He prefers a soft bed and Nora Jean's cooking, he says. But he did indicate that the two of them would try to come this way during Christmas week. Said he wanted to 'show that smarty-mouthed Boston boy how to harmonize all proper like.'" Isaac squinted and pursed his lips into a sour posture. "I'm sure he meant on the carols we will sing."

"Harmonize? Simon Keats? Why, he couldn't hold an accurate pitch if you handed it to him in a buckskin bag." Sun smiled.

"Perhaps you are right, but what Simon's singing voice lacks in sonority is mitigated by enthusiasm." All laughed in agreement.

Chapter 24

Day before the Hunt

Sun had ridden to the Jacobson cabin to finalize plans for the hunt. Anna and Marybeth scurried around the hearth, preparing pies and bread. Isaac stirred about in the pole barn, his eyes intermittently falling and weighing heavily on that big hickory up the hill. He walked quietly.

"Good morning, Patience. It's Isaac. But you know that. I haven't been here in a while. I apologize, but Marybeth and I are now married. You know that as well. I love her. And Patience, I love you. I always will. But God has given me another opportunity in this life to love again. It's good, Patience; very good. God has healed much of my broken heart through Marybeth. I guess we can love again after loss. Maybe it's not exactly the same; maybe it shouldn't be. But it is a healing and healthy love, just like that I shared with you. And I thank you – for that love and life and for your understanding. Most of all and until I leave this world, I thank God. Two wonderful and nurturing women in one lifetime is more than a man deserves. But God is good, Patience. God is good."

*****

"Isaac, are you about ready?" Sun saw Isaac walking along the creek edge below the house. "Everything is set. We need to be at the Jacobson's early morning tomorrow. Have the ladies finished baking?"

"Hello, Sun. Yes, as Simon Keats would say, 'I was born ready.' How are the Jacobsons? I guess Webster is ready for the hunt."

"They are fine, and Webster is ready. So is Oscar McDougall. The boys may go with us." Sun was affable. It seemed this was the first time in quite a while that he could be considered good company. That beast of anger, coupled with an unforgiving spirit, had consumed him. Perhaps his monsters were growing weary, were willing to leave him to recovery. He hoped they were anyway.

"Good; good. I am looking forward to the hunt and the fellowship. Tomorrow early you say?"

"Yes. We need to leave here well before sunrise. I'll have the wagon and team ready. We'll gather our flinters, the baked goods and the ladies and head out as quickly as we are loaded. It should be a good day or two of hunting and socializing." Sun exuded exhilaration.

"And work. Don't leave out the work that goes along with the socializing. Caring for and preparing meat and rendering grease is pure and simple hard work. If only Simon makes an appearance to verify we do everything to his liking!" Isaac showed exhilaration as well.

"Indeed. Things are just not the same when Simon is absent."

*****

The Hunt

Daylight was becoming a reality when Marybeth, Anna, Isaac and Sun arrived at Webster and Prudence Jacobson's cabin. Puffs of smoke rose from the nostrils of docile horses as they pulled the wagon into the Jacobson yard. Similar puffs erupted from the four humans in the wagon.

"We and the horses share that same air God gave and produce those same wafting puffs of fog. His creation is marvelous." Anna proffered a sleepy smile.

"That it is." Isaac reined the horses to a stop. "Marvelous."

"Hello all." Webster Jacobson stepped from the porch. "Climb down and go inside. Coffee is ready and a warm fire blazing. Prudence is waiting. You ladies can rest after we go for the hunt. Oscar and Matilda will be here presently." All obliged. "A shame Simon couldn't join us." Webster closed the door behind him.

"We were discussing Simon on the way out here. He is quite the character." Sun propped his big York .54 in the corner.

"He is that. I think highly of Simon Keats." Webster took his shooting pouch from a wall peg. "I think I just heard the McDougalls ride up." A knock. "Come on in. The ones of you who are old enough, have some coffee. We'll get going soon for the hunt."

Isaac was eager. He walked to the hearth, then to the door – even opened that door to peer outside. "Daylight's wasting, gentlemen. Shall we proceed? These ladies would likely appreciate our absence this early morning."

"Indeed we would." Anna poked a gentle finger into Sun's chest. "We would appreciate practically anything other than a group of grown men, and the boys of course, strutting around like young bucks trying to determine which among them is king of the herd. So, off with you. We have matters of great import to discuss."

"Yes; yes." The men offered a simultaneous response.

"We will be back by dark. If Simon were here, this entire affair would be finished before noon, he being the 'smartsome, skilledful hunter' that he claims. But since he is not, we must struggle against all odds and muddle through this chore half prepared and unschooled in such matters as making meat. But we shall persevere." Webster struck the stance of a statue, his hand tucked between the buttons of his weskit.

*****

Even without Simon, these hunters – Isaac, Oscar, Sun, Webster, the boys – proved quite adroit. First, Sun's York .54 – a fat six-point buck. And there was a spike bull elk for Oscar. Issac added a doe to Sun's buck. Webster collected the bear. This was ample for grease, bear bacon, jerked meat and roasts for all four families. Yes, they would have to collect small game along during winter, but this was all the bigger animals they would take from God's bounty. Waste was no option.

*****

"A flutter in your belly?" Marybeth asked.

"Yes, but I feel better now." Anna only half smiled; her eyes were sad. "I told Sun it was just his presence that gave me butterflies. I thought I was about to come down with some stomach ailment, but that was several days back. Really, I feel well. Please don't worry."

"I have a flutter in my belly every time I think of Liam." Lizza McDougall was enjoying her time with the women. Her younger sisters were playing hopscotch outside. "Just the thought of him and I am…."

"Oh, shush, Lizza. Goodnees me. You are hopeless. I don't know what the Reverend Sullivan will ever do with you." Matilda McDougall feigned embarrassment.

"Well, I tell you one thing Reverend Sullivan – L-i-a-m – can do with me." His name slipped from her lips with seductive smoothness. "He can...."

"Lizza McDougall. You stop that. We all will be blushing if you keep this up." Matilda's embarrassment was no longer feigned. "Not even married and talking such things. Goodness me."

"Better to talk such things before marriage than to...." Lizza twirled a strand of hair, wiggled her fingers as if flying and giggled loudly. The others gave in and joined her glee.

"You are right, Matilda. Liam Sullivan won't know what to do with her." Anna found enough breath to speak.

"I will be glad to show him." Lizza was not willing to give her comrades a respite.

"Now when is your wedding?" Prudence asked. "I say it simply must be soon." More laughter.

*****

"Well, look at that!" Matilda sounded shocked. All the women looked up from their preparations for cooking down grease and salting bear bacon.

"I can hardly believe the men are back so soon. Barely noon now." Prudence was surprised but happy just the same.

"Hello hunters. I see Simon joined you after all." Anna teased them.

"No, he didn't come. We weren't expecting him." Webster Jacobson was a literal thinker. "Why do you say that about Simon?"

"Oh, since you were missing the 'smartsome, skilledful hunter,' we anticipated this would be an all-day doing. In fact, you said the same earlier. Said you would be back about dark – or something like that. And here you are, long before dark. Did you boys give up and just come staggering back?" Anna was incessant.

Sun caught her jest first and began to snicker. "Anna Walker Bain, you know that I am next in line to the most 'smartsome, skilledful hunter in these here parts; shorely am,' so why would you expect anything other than an early return from a successful hunt? We have enough grease and jerked meat and roasts for all the families. The bear roasts will be wonderful Now while we take the wagon and retrieve all this meat, you ladies get those fires and pots ready. We have a making-meat party tonight." There was joy and laughter on the frontier.

Chapter 25

Thanksgiving

"A grand meal, Marybeth." Anna hugged her step-mother. "This is a wonderful time of year, and sharing the time with you and Isaac in your home is the crown of this day. And with you and Nora Jean, Simon. Any day or season or event is enriched by your company."

"Thank you, Anna. And Marybeth, thank you and Isaac as well." Nora Jean didn't allow Simon an opportunity to speak after Anna expressed her sentiments.

"Shorely was good; shorely was." Simon found – or made - his opening. "I ain't much on speechifyin' as you all know, but I gotta agree with Miss Anna and Nora Jean that this here was one dandy meal and a plumb specialfied kinda gatherin' of smartsome folks. Shorely was. Why I remember...."

"Easy Simon. We don't particularly care about what you re-member, at the moment anyway." Nora Jean made a failed attempt to thwart Simon's ever-present rattling. "And what on earth is speechif-yin' and specialfied, Simon? What language is that?"

"Oh, that there's the right kinda language, the kind what's gonna reach right out there and tug all them what listen in right close like so's they can hear smartsome and dignifidy words. Shorely is. And iffin you all don't mind, I think I'll jest go right on ahead with my speecifiyin' even iffin I ain't much on doing such things as that."

"Goodness, Simon. Must you embarrass me and torture others every chance you get? What shall I do to tame your obnoxious manners?" Nora Jean was not nearly so annoyed as she pretended.

"Shorely don't mean to 'barrass or torture; shorely don't. My 'pologies. It's jest that I get so thrillified and such when I'm with smartsome folk like this that I gotta spread more smartsomes and rake in some smartsomes from ever'body else. Shorely do. And reckonin' what you gonna do with me, Nora Jean, I suggest that you jest keep on a' lovin' me like I know you do and me keep on a' lovin' you like you know I do and ever'thing's jest gonna be smooth as creek water. Smooth, I tell you."

"Well said, Simon, Well said." Sun bowed in Simon's direction. "And I was surprised and sad that you didn't join us awhile back when we made meat. The hunt would have been more interesting, I should say entertaining, had you been there."

"Shorely woulda'; Shorely woulda'. My 'pologies. I know you all needed me, what with bein' the skilledful hunter and all like I am, but I jest sorta' wanted to stay 'round close to the cabin. Soft bed, Nora Jean's cookin' – and Nora Jean for that matter. You gent'men know what I'm a' talkin' 'bout. Anyhow, I 'spect I done the right thing, what with lettin' you all get some huntin' smartsome through 'xperience instead 'uh havin' me there to feed it to you from a carved cedar spoon. More learnified that way. Don't forget so quick like when learnin' comes from 'xpereince." Simon slapped his knee and rolled in boisterous laughter.

"Yes; you are probably right, Simon." Isaac entered the conversation. "Still, it would have been good to have you."

"Shorely would; yessiree. 'Spect you gent'men went 'round them there hills grievin' 'cause I warn't there."

"Well, I wouldn't say grieving." Sun this time. "We were more pleased than pained."

"Ain't so. Ain't so a'tall. Say, did I ever tell you 'bout that there buffler hunt I took all by my lonesome and…?"

"Do you mean the one where you fell in the creek or where the catamount chased you out of that cave or the one…?" Sun was suddenly interrupted.

"Yeah, them too, but not them this time. I'm a' talkin' 'bout 'nother time. Well you see, I was all by my lonesome…."

"Simon, no one wants to hear embellishments and half-truths about your hunting prowess. So just be quiet and let someone else talk." Nora Jean mildly scolded.

"Naw, ain't no 'bellishments and shorely is the plumb truth; shorely is. And I 'spect ever'body's jest deep innersted in my huntin' tales since I'm so skilledful and all."

"I doubt there is much interest, but if you must, please do get on with it and then fall silent so that someone else can get in the occasional word. Now dear husband, on with your story. We, I am sure, will be enriched and will absolutely be ready for someone else to speak by the time you are finished."

"Thank you Nora Jean. And like I's a' sayin'; I needed some buffler meat, shorely did. 'Bout starved out there in the Middle Ground. Needed me a buffler hide too. Winter was a' comin' and I'd done plumb wore out ever'thing I had. Warn't nothin' in my little ole half face 'septin' some straw and a pot for boilin'. Done got dire, I tell you.

"Anyhow, here I was all by my lonesome when I come up on this here buffler 'bout five miles downhill from the half-face. 'Coursein' I don't never miss, so 'fore I knowed it I had me a buffler. Started cuttin' that rascal in quarters, all the while takin' plumb good care of that hide. Needed that hide whole, shorely did. And…."

"All by yourself you were? Skinning and quartering a buffalo? By yourself?" Sun pressed Simon.

"All by my lonesome; shorely was. So as I was a' sayin'; I got them quarters and that hide offin' and had to figger out how to git it all to my half-face. So I jest wrapped them quarters and the hump meat in that hide, cut me a saplin', tied ever'thing to that saplin', slung the whole load over my shoulders and struck out up them there hills."

"Simon, that would have weighed 400 pounds I'd guess. And you carried that load on your shoulders five miles to the half-face – uphill?" Sun was a touch indignant.

"Yessiree; shorely did. And it was the longest, hardest five miles I done ever walked!" That knee slap and boisterous laughter again.

"Then there was this here time when I needed myself a bear and…."

"Enough, Simon. Now stop your chatter." Nora Jean frowned slightly.

"Naw, this here hunt was more thrillinfied than that there buffler doings. I needed me a bear – grease, bacon, roasts, hide. Needed it bad. Tough times again. So I found me a bear – up there close to Middle Ground. Had me 'nother half-face by then.

"Well, this here bear, he spied me 'fore I could git a shot, and tore out a' runnin' like his tail was on fire. I lit out behind him. This here bear, a fat rascal – just what I needed – run plumb inside a gapin' holler of a broad beech and clumb six feet 'fore he run outta room. Shorely did. When I got there he was a' backin' down real slow like, gittin' ready to tear out sommers else, but I stood right there like a stump at that gapin' openin'.

"That there bear, he'd sneakiefy down and then back up – down and back up. It was gittin' late in the day and dark was shorely comin' soon; shorely was. Warn't no way I could handle a bear in the black dark of them there woods and hills. I figgered I had me a problem, but Simon Keats ani't never been one to hustle off away from trouble. 'Sides, I shorely needed me a bear. I hatched me a plan.

"I curled up real tight like 'gainst that gapin' holler and stuck my feet inside so's I could feel that bear if he sneakiefied down.. Just decided to spend the night with that bear and me and him meet up at daybreak to talk things over. Shorely didn't git much sleep that night, what with that there bear sneakiefyin' down and back up – down and back up. But shorely was the best bear bacon I ever et. And still got that big ole hide. Saved me from freezin' plumb to death plenty a' times. Shorely did."

"All right, Simon. Enough. I've had all your outrageous tales I can endure for one day. Four hundred pounds of meat and hide; a night with your feet in a tree hollow that is occupied by a bear. Enough. Do you think me – all these here – foolish?" Sun stared, but a kind and loving stare. More in humor than in reprimand.

"I'd think you foolish only iffin you'd a' been there and done that." Simon roared and slapped his knee. "You all jest love ole Simon Keats, don't you?"

Chapter 26

Boston – Early December

Martha Bain sat silently. Simple reflection or melancholy? She was not certain. What was certain is that she missed Anna and Sun. Missed Squire as well. That early Squire anyway - that Squire she fell in love with and raised her children with and depended upon and admired. Admired for a very long time, but admiration had morphed into misery.

Had she forgiven? She most assuredly had not forgotten. Every day that ache, that menacing torment creeping serpent-like, painting a weaving and hideous trail of the past. No, she had not forgotten. And some days the recall was numbing. Fingertips, shoulders, legs, even heart and mind – numb. Had Squire actually done what she thought he had done? Yes. Then numb again.

Her thoughts. *A letter to those I love is in order. Will it be my last? Perhaps; perhaps not. But a letter I will write. Share my thoughts, my wishes and hopes for them all and my thanks for them being who and what they are. A letter from my heart, my mind, my inner core. If these don't suddenly become numb.* Parchment and quill and ink bowl at hand, Martha Bain wrote:

Dearest Children:

I write to you what could possibly be my last letter. And know from the very beginning that when I refer to you as my children, I include all – spouses, grandchildren, all. You are my children, my dear, dear children. How blessed I have been to share my life with you. All you have been a pure joy and continue as such. Oh, the sweet memories.

Cassie and Cora, you were adorable babies and beautiful little girls. Now you are beautiful young women, both inside and out. That inside beauty is even more essential than that which is on the outside. That is the way it should be.

Yes, there was the occasional squabble when you were little girls, these generally sparked by insignificant matters such as who would sit where. But those matters were not insignificant then, not to you at least. But matters like that pale into oblivion when set beside the grown-up challenges of life.

And there was the occasional occurrence of more serious encounters that terminated with hair pulling and raised voices. I remember those well. Tears flowed, at times profusely. But I remember most those apologies and hugs and resumed relationships of sisters - loving, caring sisters.

Now you are adults. There is no hair pulling in your disagreements now, is there? If so, I am not aware of it. Of course there is not. You are mature; you walk with the strength of God and His love. You handle such obstacles as adults should handle them – with understanding and respect and graciousness. I pray that will always be, and I have full confidence that it will.

Jackson, you, like your sisters, were an adorable baby. That may seem out of place to you now, but you were. Chubby, always smiling, constantly winning hearts of all who held and cuddled you. Perhaps

I would do well to ask Anna if that is how she sees you, but I fear the truth. Not really. I have no doubts. But in all that adorable and heart-winning charm you exemplified, I must say that you were often insufferable! Now before you frown and think poorly of me, I must explain.

You were the dreamer, the poet, the spirit that would not be conquered – other than by God, of course. Your mind seemed always on the exotic, the world beyond that with which you were familiar. You opted to expand your boundaries, and you continue with that same propensity. Still, you so very much loved. Loved all of us and others. For all that I say you have my admiration.

Spouses of my birth children, I did not have the privilege of watching you grow up. But I now know your hearts. They are sound, grounded. I respect the way you love those you married, how you care for your children. My admiration goes to you as well. You, as my own, have blessed my life.

Now as I close this letter, I admonish all of you to hold firm in your faith, grow in the Word, stay in tune with God. I challenge you to seek His will daily and follow that will with vigor. Speak love, but more importantly, live love. And when troubles come, and they will certainly come, stand. Look to God. Troubles will pass; blessings will endure. I love you all.

Your Mother,
Martha Bain

Martha's letter would not be opened until the reading of her last will and testament.

*****

Wedding in the Settlement

The wedding of Lizza McDougall and Reverend Liam Sullivan was, like that of Marybeth and Isaac, simple but beautiful. Proper it was. Friday late afternoon, dusk. The sunset positively grand. Orange and pink and light scarlet. And gentle. Lizza fairly bubbled. Reverend Sullivan found it impossible to keep his eyes off her. The visiting minister pronounced them husband and wife and allowed that Reverend Sullivan should kiss his bride. Lizza practically smothered the Good Reverend.

There were immediate cheers, but these turned to throat clearing and soft coughing and whispers before Lizza released her hold. *You reckon the Reverend will ever preach again?* A whisper, a too-loud whisper, crept from somewhere in the back. Mrs. Franklinton squirmed. Festivities began shortly afterward outside and in front of the church, as these had with Marybeth and Isaac.

"Well, I don't suppose we should expect you to fill the pulpit day after tomorrow, Reverend." Mrs. Franklinton had stopped to congratulate or scrutinize or criticize the newlyweds. She nor they were sure which. "Young man, this has been scandalous. It was indeed time you stopped this charade of innocence and become at least legal – if not fully acceptable. Still, scandalous I tell you."

"Oh no, Mrs. Franklinton. Reverend Sullivan – Liam – will not be available this Sunday. The visiting Reverend will, however, and I feel certain he will bring a rousing sermon. Perhaps about the sins of gossip and being judgmental and a host of other infractions. Will you be in attendance?

"Additionally, Liam will be a changed man before then. You may not even recognize him. He will be weary and worn, wearing a smile that no one can sweep away even with a corn-shuck broom like I am sure you have. No, he will be in no condition to preach so soon after this wedding. Good to see you again, Mrs. Franklinton." Lizza terminated her speech with a wave of dismissal.

"Well, I never." Mrs. Franklinton huffed.

"Probably not, Mrs. Franklinton. Probably not." Liam seemed to have developed some rare form of courage.

*****

There was much merriment. Food, a bonfire, dancing. At some point Lizza and Liam were seen walking hand-in-hand toward Reverend Sullivan's modest cottage, Lizza giggling and teasing. They would leave the following day for a two-week adventure.

"Reverend Sullivan best make ready, Anna. His eyes will be opened to a brand new world soon." Sun smiled at Anna.

"As yours were, Sun?"

"Indeed; as mine were." He held Anna tightly.

Chapter 27

Walker Cabin-Week before Christmas

"It is over, Anna."

"Over? What is over?"

"I should say many rather than it, for many were my transgressions. My anger; my lack of forgiveness; my failure to trust. Over. Behind me. Perhaps these or others similar will come again as life presents its twists and turns, but the recent struggles are over. God has forgiven me; I have forgiven Father. I am no longer angry at him, at those men who attacked us, at myself. No longer angry."

"A blessed recognition, Sun. Prayers have been answered. I rejoice and celebrate with you."

"And I thank you. Your strength played a key role in all this. God and you."

"But let's not forget that I have been angry, disillusioned, downcast. The list is long. But I have healed a great deal. I no longer wrestle with those issues as I did just two months back. Sun, we have so very much to be thankful for, and living in the past or in dread or in fear or in any number of other debilitating maladies is of no value. We forgive, release, trust, love, move forward with God as our guide and strength. We move forward."

"Yes. We move forward. The future is uncertain, even frightening. But we move under God's leadership. Please, walk with me. Let's go to the creek, the holly tree."

"The holly tree, Sun? Isn't the memory from there painful?"

"Oh, a bit. You refused my advances there, admirable though they were if I recall. But it is not painful. It was there that I fully knew I was in love with you. It was there that I helped you break boughs with berries to be used to decorate the cabin. Not painful at all. Rather refreshing I would say. Walk with me."

"Yes, of course. Anywhere you choose. I shall be by your side."

"And I by your side, Anna."

"Sun, do you remember the story of Esther?" The two of them were at the creek edge now.

"Vaguely, but you are more the Bible student than I. Please outline that story."

"Not in its entirety, but I will give you the core of it."

"Yes, please."

"Esther was married to the King. Plans were progressing to eliminate the Jews - Esther's family and others. Although Esther was Queen, she had no license to enter the King's court without his permission. Her uncle Mordecai encouraged her to approach the King with a plea to spare those condemned. Oh, and she was a very beautiful woman." Anna smiled.

"As beautiful as you?"

"Now, now. But whatever you say. You think too highly of me."

"Never."

"Esther was deeply afraid. The King had authority to have her or anyone else executed if protocol were breached, such as entering his presence without his express permission, and even she, the

King's beautiful wife, was subject to that ruling. But God's leadership through Esther's uncle gave her strength."

"And the King had her executed, along with all her kin folk?" Sun teased but not irreverently.

"No, no. She won the King over to her side. Remember, God was in this thing all along. I see this story as one that teaches us to follow God even in the face of fear, even in the face of death. To use what we have, in this case Esther's great beauty, for God's purposes. And while it is true that we will not be delivered from every situation, we will be comforted and strengthened, even rewarded for following God. That is what I want us to do – individually and as husband and wife. Follow fearlessly, diligently. Even when we can't see the road ahead. Follow. Follow God."

"Yes, I concur. And since we are discussing matters of grave import, I need to tell you that I have considered enlisting in the struggle for freedom when we return to Boston."

"I am not surprised, Sun. I would have expected nothing less. But I must know that you are convinced that this is God's leading."

"Of a certainty. This might not be in the capacity of bearing arms and going to battle, but again that is a possibility. It could be supporting the effort in some other form. I will just have to pray, seek out advice regarding that element of service. But yes, I believe God is leading."

"Then I support you. Like Esther, I will be afraid. But also like Esther, I will face, not the King but the situation, with courage – courage that comes directly from our Heavenly Father. Yes, I support you, Sun."

"Then it is settled?"

"Yes, Sun; it is settled. I love you."

"And I love you, Anna. Now, may we turn our attention to a less complicated line of thinking and gather greenery for the cabin. I cannot imagine a Christmas minus greenery. And you decorate a cabin splendidly. We want it looking cheery when Marybeth and Isaac come for Christmas dinner. But promise not to refuse my advances in the event I contemplate such an action."

"I promise." They walked closely and smiled.

*****

Christmas

The Walker Cabin was perfectly decorated. Pine cones, bulbous and bulking, blanketed the mantle. Bright holly berries twinkled from crevasses in those cones. Boughs from that holly, along with fragrant pine needles, created a runner along the worn oak table. Just to one side and near the hearth, a small cedar stood proudly, emitting its own sweet aroma. It hosted at its peak a hand-sized star Isaac carved for Anna and Patience many years past. We can't have Christmas without the star, Anna recalled her mother saying.

And there were candles. Everywhere. Not just those used for the customary chore of chasing darkness from a room; there were far too many for that simple task. These, fabricated for this express purpose, were in every window, on every shelf, on the table and in hand-made sconces along the walls. In multiples these candles were. Everywhere. Poured from bee's wax, they would contribute mightily to the smells of Christmas once lighted for the evening.

The mistletoe? Anna planned that judiciously. Four fist-sized bundles dangled from thin strips of buckskin, placed strategically so that no one who entered would be immune. Marybeth and Isaac would be along directly, spend the night and stay for a true frontier Christmas celebration.

*****

Christmas Day. All woke slowly but soon stirred. Hot coffee, biscuits, fruit jam, and crisp bear bacon were served. Isaac and Sun took a brief walk along the creek. The chill, while not objectionable, required a greatcoat. Anna and Marybeth sat beside the hearth.

"I think that could be a possibility." Anna was reflective. "I have been praying about that for months."

"Yes, and I think the same with me. I can't say I've prayed that it would happen, but all things are in God's control. If He wills, I shall oblige." Marybeth patted Anna's hand.

*****

"Good morning again, ladies." Isaac proffered a small bow as he and Sun entered the cabin. "This is a grand day. Sun and I walked along the creek and surroundings were glorious."

"Indeed. Though the oaks and hickories and sweetgums were austere, even skeletal, they were perfect for the season. They remind me of renewal, for they will renew and put on leaves come early spring. Much like life, I would say." Sun was his usual poetic self.

"I agree. " Isaac smiled. "Sun, I will need your assistance a bit later. We need to prepare the fire and get meat ready for supper. There is no rush, but we can't be delinquent or Christmas supper will run late. Don't want that to happen because we have a tremendous amount of singing to do after supper. And since Simon couldn't come, we must also do that boisterous and off-key singing ourselves."

"Truly sorry he won't be with us. That will leave a tremendous cavern in the celebrations. But yes, of course, I shall gladly assist you, Isaac."

"Anna, Sun, Isaac, I need to make an announcement. Don't be concerned; the news is good. But I have waited so that my suspicions could be confirmed. I think it wise to have my say now." Marybeth looked gently into the eyes of each.

"Marybeth, is something wrong?" Isaac showed alarm.

"Goodness no, Isaac. I would say all is right. So I shall get to the point. Isaac Walker, you are going to be a father again. Anna Walker Bain, you are going to have a baby brother or sister." Silence was thick; mouths were open; eyes were wide and glittering. And then a mass cheer. Everyone at once – talking and congratulating. Sun slapped Isaac's back.

"I can hear Simon Keats now: 'That Isaac Walker shorely is somethin'; he shorely is.'"

"Yes he is, surely something." Anna was giddy. "Congratulations to you both. I love you."

"Oh my." Isaac had no other words, but his smile assumed the posture of a permanent fixture.

"And while we are congratulating and celebrating, and certainly not to diminish this incredible news just brought, I would like to say something as well." Anna had full attention of all.

"Say it, Anna. What is your news?" Isaac was intrigued.

"Sun, I just need to advise you that while making plans for a trip to Boston or anything else, you will need to consider your child." Anna touched his cheek gently and smiled.

"My child? My child? What are you saying, Anna? Our child?"

"Yes. Right here and growing just fine, thank you." Anna patted her belly. "I wasn't sure until now, but there is no question. You, like Isaac, are going to be a father." More cheers and smiles and congratulations.

"I can just hear Simon Keats now." Isaac gained the floor: "'That Jackson Bain shorely is somethin'; shorely is.' And I agree with

Simon. My sincere congratulations Anna, Sun. I love you."

The afternoon sentiment was blithe. They sang Christmas songs long into the night.

END